PENGUIN CLASSICS

Maigret at the Coron‹

'I love reading Simenon. He makes me think of Che...
– William Faulkner

'A truly wonderful writer . . . marvellously readable – lucid, simple, absolutely in tune with the world he creates'
– Muriel Spark

'Few writers have ever conveyed with such a sure touch, the bleakness of human life'
– A. N. Wilson

'One of the greatest writers of the twentieth century . . . Simenon was unequalled at making us look inside, though the ability was masked by his brilliance at absorbing us obsessively in his stories'
– *Guardian*

'A novelist who entered his fictional world as if he were part of it'
– Peter Ackroyd

'The greatest of all, the most genuine novelist we have had in literature'
– André Gide

'Superb . . . The most addictive of writers . . . A unique teller of tales'
– *Observer*

'The mysteries of the human personality are revealed in all their disconcerting complexity'
– Anita Brookner

'A writer who, more than any other crime novelist, combined a high literary reputation with popular appeal'– P. D. James

'A supreme writer . . . Unforgettable vividness' – *Independent*

'Compelling, remorseless, brilliant'
– John Gray

'Extraordinary masterpieces of the twentieth century'
– John Banville

GEORGES SIMENON

Maigret at the Coroner's

Translated by LINDA COVERDALE

PENGUIN BOOKS

PENGUIN CLASSICS

UK | USA | Canada | Ireland | Australia
India | New Zealand | South Africa

Penguin Books is part of the Penguin Random House group of companies
whose addresses can be found at global.penguinrandomhouse.com.

Penguin
Random House
UK

First published in French as *Maigret chez le coroner* by Presses de la Cité 1949
This translation first published 2016
002

Typeset in Dante MT Std by Palimpsest Book Production Ltd, Falkirk, Stirlingshire
Printed in Great Britain by Clays Ltd, St Ives plc

ISBN: 978-0-241-20681-2

www.greenpenguin.co.uk

MIX
Paper from
responsible sources
FSC
www.fsc.org
FSC® C018179

Penguin Random House is committed to a
sustainable future for our business, our readers
and our planet. This book is made from Forest
Stewardship Council® certified paper.

Contents

1. Maigret, Deputy Sheriff 1

2. At the Head of the Class 21

3. The Little Chinese Fellow Who Did Not Drink 40

4. The Man Who Wound Clocks 62

5. The Driver's Deposition 84

6. The Parade of Pals 104

7. The Inspector's Questions 125

8. The Black Man Speaks Up 145

9. The Sergeant's Hip Flask 162

1. Maigret, Deputy Sheriff

'Hey, you!'

Maigret turned around, as if at school, to see who was being singled out.

'Yes, you, over there . . .'

And the gaunt old man with the immense white moustache, who seemed sprung full-blown from the Bible, pointed with a trembling arm. At whom? Maigret looked at his neighbours: a man; a woman. Abashed, he finally realized that everyone – including the coroner, the Air Force sergeant on the witness stand, the jurors, the sheriffs, the attorney – was looking at him.

'Me?' he asked, apparently ready to stand up, astonished that they would have need of him.

All those faces were smiling, however, as if he were the only person not in on some joke.

'Yes,' intoned the old man, who looked like Ezekiel – and Clemenceau, too. 'Put out your pipe and be quick about it!'

He couldn't even remember lighting it. Embarrassed, he sat back down, mumbling apologies as his neighbours laughed in a friendly way.

It was not a dream. He was wide awake. It was he, Detective Chief Inspector Maigret of the Police Judiciaire, sitting there more than 10,000 kilometres from Paris, attending an inquest held by a coroner wearing neither jacket nor waistcoat yet looking as grave and well mannered as a bank clerk.

In truth, he was perfectly aware that his colleague, Agent Cole of the FBI, had delicately got rid of him, but Maigret could not manage to feel offended: he would have done the same in the other man's place. And hadn't he done just that two years earlier in France, when chaperoning his colleague Mr Pyke, of Scotland Yard, and had he not often left him on some café terrace, the way you deposit an umbrella in a cloakroom, and told him with a reassuring smile, 'I'll be back in just a moment . . .'

Except that the Americans were more welcoming. In New York as well as in the ten or eleven other states he had travelled through so far, everyone would clap him on the shoulder.

'What's your first name?'

He could hardly tell them he didn't have one! He had to admit that his name was Jules. The other man would mull that over for a moment.

'Oh! Yes . . . Julius!'

They pronounced it 'Joulious', which seemed to him already somewhat improved.

'Have a drink, Julius!'

And so all along his journey, in many a bar, he had downed innumerable beers and Manhattans and whiskies.

He had already been drinking that day, before lunch, with the mayor of Tucson and the county sheriff, to whom he had been introduced by Harry Cole.

What amazed him the most was not so much his

surroundings or the people but himself, or, rather, the fact that he, Maigret, was here in a city in Arizona and that for the moment, for example, he was sitting on a bench in a small room presided over by a justice of the peace.

Although they had had drinks before lunch, iced water had been served with the meal itself. The mayor had been quite pleasant. As for the sheriff, he had handed him a little piece of paper and the handsome silver badge of a deputy sheriff, like the ones seen in cowboy films.

It was the eighth or ninth badge he had received that way: he was already a deputy in eight or nine counties in New Jersey, Maryland, Virginia, North or South Carolina (he could no longer remember which), Texas – and New Orleans.

He had often welcomed foreign colleagues in Paris, but this was the first time he had undertaken such a trip, a 'study tour' they called it officially, 'to learn about American methods'.

'You ought to spend a few days in Arizona, before you get to California. It's on your way.'

It was always on his way. And that way they had him covering hundreds of miles. What these people referred to as a small detour took three or four days.

'It's just next door!'

That meant it was at least as far away as from Paris to Marseille, and sometimes he rolled along in a Pullman car for a whole day without seeing a real city.

Cole, the FBI agent, had taken charge of him in Arizona.

'Tomorrow,' he had said, 'we'll go take a look at the Mexican border. It's right in the neighbourhood.'

This time, that meant only about 100 kilometres away.

'Nogales will interest you. It's a border town, straddling both countries, and most of the marijuana passes through here.'

Maigret had learned that marijuana, a Mexican plant, was slowly making inroads on opium and cocaine with drug addicts.

'Nogales is also the exit point for most of the cars stolen in California.'

In the meantime, though, Harry Cole had sidelined him. He must have had something else to do that afternoon.

'It so happens there's a coroner's inquest today. Would you like to sit in on it?'

He had taken Maigret and parked him on one of the three benches in the little room with white walls. An American flag hung behind the justice of the peace, who doubled as a coroner. Without telling his French colleague that he would be leaving him on his own, Cole had gone off to shake some hands and pat a few shoulders.

Then he had passed by to say casually, 'I'll be back to get you later.'

Maigret knew nothing about the matter before the court. No one in the room was wearing a jacket. True, the temperature was around 45°C. The six jurors were sitting on the same bench as he was but at the other end, over by the door, and they included a black man, an Indian with a strong jaw, a Mexican who looked a bit like both of them, and a middle-aged woman wearing a flowered dress and a hat perched strangely forwards on her head.

Now and then Ezekiel would get up and try to adjust

the huge ceiling fan, which made so much noise that it was hard to hear people's voices.

Things seemed to be toddling along nicely. In France, Maigret would have said '*à la papa*'. Up on a dais, the coroner was wearing an immaculate white shirt with a floral-patterned silk tie.

The witness, or the accused – Maigret wasn't exactly sure – was seated on a chair nearby. He was an Air Force sergeant, in a beige twill uniform. There were four more like him, lined up facing the jury, and they looked like overgrown schoolboys.

'Tell us what happened on the evening of July 27.'

The man addressed was Sergeant Ward, whose name Maigret had already heard mentioned. He was at least 1.85 metres tall, with blue eyes beneath thick black eyebrows that met above his nose.

'I went to pick up Bessie at her place at around seven thirty.'

'Louder. Turn towards the jury. Can you hear, jurors?'

They indicated that they could not. Sergeant Ward coughed to clear his throat.

'I went to pick up Bessie at her place at around seven thirty.'

Maigret had to listen with extra care, because he had had almost no occasion to speak English since his schooldays. Words were escaping him, and he found some expressions baffling.

'You are married and have two children?'

'Yes, sir.'

'How long have you known Bessie Mitchell?'

The sergeant sat thinking, like a good pupil preparing to answer a teacher's question. At one point, he glanced over at someone sitting next to Maigret, who had no idea yet who the man was.

'Six weeks.'

'Where did you first meet her?'

'In a drive-in place where she was a carhop.'

Maigret had become familiar with drive-ins. His official escorts would often stop, especially in the evenings, at small roadside eateries. They would stay in the car, and a young woman would come over to take their order, then bring them sandwiches, hot dogs or spaghetti on a window tray that hooked on to the outside of the car door.

'Did you have sexual relations with her?'

'Yes, sir.'

'That same evening?'

'Yes, sir.'

'Where did this happen?'

'In the car. We parked out in the desert.'

The desert, cacti and sand, began at the city limits. Patches of desert even survived among some neighbourhoods in Tuscon.

'Did you see her often after that evening?'

'About three times a week.'

'And each time you'd have relations with her?'

'No, sir.'

Maigret almost expected the punctilious little judge to ask, 'Why is that?'

But his question was, 'How many times, then?'

'Once a week.'

And only Maigret smiled slightly at that.

'Always out in the desert?'

'Out there and at her place.'

'She lived alone?'

Sergeant Ward searched among the faces of those sitting on the benches and pointed out a young woman sitting to Maigret's left.

'She lived with Erna Bolton.'

'What did you do, on 27 July, after you picked up Bessie Mitchell at her place?'

'I drove her to the Penguin Bar, where my friends were waiting for me.'

'What friends?'

This time the sergeant pointed to the four other soldiers in Air Force uniforms, giving their names one by one.

'Dan Mullins, Jimmy Van Fleet, O'Neil and Wo Lee.'

This last was a Chinese youth who looked barely sixteen.

'Was there anyone else with you at the Penguin?'

'No, sir. Not at our table.'

'Were there people at another table?'

'There was Bessie's brother, Harold Mitchell.'

This was the man just to the right of Maigret. The inspector had already noticed a large boil below his neighbour's ear.

'Was he alone?'

'No. With Erna Bolton, the musician and Maggie.'

'How old was Bessie Mitchell?'

'She'd told me she was twenty-three.'

'Did you know that she was really only seventeen years old and therefore too young to drink legally in a bar?'

'No, sir.'

'You're sure her brother didn't tell you that?'

'He told me later, at the musician's place, when she began drinking whisky straight from the bottle. He told me he didn't want anyone giving his sister drinks, that she was a minor and that he was the one who had been made her guardian.'

'Were you unaware that Bessie had been married and divorced?'

'No, sir. I knew.'

'Had you promised her to marry her?'

Sergeant Ward clearly hesitated.

'Yes, sir.'

'You wanted to get a divorce to marry her?'

'I had told her I would do that.'

In the doorway was a big deputy sheriff – a colleague! – wearing dull yellow cotton duck trousers, a shirt unbuttoned at the neck and a leather belt full of cartridges. An enormous horn-handled revolver hung over one buttock.

'Did you all have drinks together?'

'Yes, sir.'

'Did you have a lot to drink? About how many glasses of beer?'

Ward closed his eyes for a moment to think about this.

'I didn't keep count. Judging from the rounds, maybe fifteen or twenty.'

'Each?'

Ward calmly replied, 'Yes, sir. And a few whiskies besides.'

The curious thing was, no one seemed particularly surprised.

'It was at the Penguin that you had an argument with Bessie's brother?'

'Yes, sir.'

'Is it true that he reproached you for having relations with his sister, and you a married man?'

'No, sir.'

'He never reproached you for that? He didn't ask you to leave his sister alone?'

'No, sir.'

'Why were you arguing?'

'Because I wanted him to pay me the money he owed me.'

'Did he owe you a large amount?'

'About two dollars.'

Barely enough to cover one of those many rounds at the Penguin.

'Did you get into a fight?'

'No, sir. We went outside to settle the matter, then returned to the bar to have a drink together.'

'Were you drunk?'

'Not very, yet.'

'Did anything else happen at the Penguin?'

'No, sir.'

'In short, you were drinking. You drank until one in the morning, closing time at the bar.'

'Yes, sir.'

'Wasn't one of your pals flirting with Bessie?'

'Sergeant Mullins,' Ward admitted, after a moment.

'You spoke to him about it.'

'No. I made sure he wouldn't be next to her.'

His friend Mullins was as tall as he was, also dark-haired, a fellow whom girls must have thought good-looking and who vaguely resembled some film star, although it was hard to say which one.

'What happened at one in the morning?'

'We went to Tony's place. Tony Lacour, the musician.'

The man must have been in the courtroom, but Maigret didn't know what he looked like.

'Who paid for the two bottles of whisky you took away with you?'

'I think Wo Lee bought one of them.'

'Had he been drinking with you throughout the evening?'

'No, sir. Corporal Wo Lee does not drink or smoke. He insisted on paying for something.'

'How many rooms are there in the musician's apartment?'

'. . . A bedroom . . . a small living room . . . a bathroom and a kitchen.'

'What room were you and the others in?'

'All of them, sir.'

'In which room did you quarrel with Bessie?'

'The kitchen. We weren't quarrelling. I caught Bessie drinking whisky out of the bottle. It wasn't the first time that had happened.'

'You mean, not the first time that evening?'

'I mean that she'd done it other times before July 27. I didn't want her drinking too much because afterwards she'd be sick.'

'Bessie was alone in the kitchen?'

'She was with him.'

He jerked his chin towards Sergeant Mullins.

And now Maigret, who had been sluggish and somnolent, Maigret, who knew nothing about this case, began opening his mouth at times as if a question were burning his lips.

'Who suggested driving to Nogales to spend the rest of the night there?'

'Bessie.'

'What time was it?'

'Around three in the morning. Maybe two thirty.'

Nogales was the border town where Harry Cole wanted to take Maigret. Tucson's bars close at one a.m., but people can drink all night long on the other side of the fence.

'Who got into your car?'

'Bessie and my four pals.'

'Bessie's brother didn't go with you? Or the musician, or Erna Bolton, or Maggie Wallach either?'

'No, sir.'

'You don't know what they did?'

'No, sir.'

'When you set out, where were you all sitting in the car?'

'Bessie was up front, between me driving and Sergeant Mullins. The other three were in the back seat.'

'Didn't you stop the car shortly before crossing the city limits?'

'Yes, sir.'

'And you asked Bessie to sit elsewhere. Why?'

'So she wouldn't be next to Dan Mullins any more.'

'You had her switch places with Corporal Van Fleet and sit in the back. It was fine with you that she'd be behind your back, in the dark, with the other two?'

'Yes, sir.'

Suddenly, without any warning, the coroner announced brusquely, 'Recess!'

He rose and headed towards the neighbouring office marked 'private' on the frosted-glass door. Ezekiel pulled an enormous pipe from his pocket and, as he lit it, he shot Maigret a funny little look.

Everyone left the courtroom: the jurors, the Air Force men, the women, the few curious spectators.

The room was on the first floor of a vast building in the Spanish Colonial style, with colonnades around a patio. The jail was in one wing, while the other housed the various administrative services of the county.

The five Air Force men went to sit on a bench by the colonnade, and Maigret noticed that they were not talking among themselves. It was extremely hot. In one corner of the arcade there was a red machine where people were dropping nickels into a slot to get a bottle of Coca-Cola.

Almost everyone was going there, including the grey-haired gentleman who must have been the district attorney. They were all drinking casually from the bottle, then putting the empties into a bottle crate.

Maigret felt a little like a boy at his first playtime in a

new school, but he had stopped hoping that Harry Cole would soon come and get him.

He had never been in a courtroom before without a jacket, and this clothing question had been a problem. After crossing a certain line, somewhere around Virginia, he had understood that he could no longer spend his days in a jacket and detachable collar.

And all his life, he had worn braces. His trousers, tailored in France, came halfway up his chest.

He no longer remembered in which city one of his colleagues had marched him off to a shop and had him buy a pair of those lightweight trousers he saw all the men wearing out here, and a leather belt sporting a large silver steer-head buckle.

Other, more flamboyant customers, fresh from parts east, would dash to the store to emerge decked out head-to-toe as cowboys.

Maigret noticed that two jurors, even though they looked fairly unadventurous, were wearing high-heeled, colourfully decorated boots under their trouser legs.

The swing-out cylinder revolvers embellishing the belts of the sheriffs fascinated Maigret; they were exactly like those he'd seen in Westerns since he was a child.

'Members of the jury! Let's go!' yelled Ezekiel unceremoniously, like a teacher collecting his pupils.

He clapped his hands and then, keeping a sly eye on Maigret's pipe, he tapped out his own against his heel.

Maigret no longer felt like such a greenhorn. He returned to his seat, the only difference being that Harold Mitchell, the brother with the boil below his ear, and

Erna Bolton, whom he had unwittingly separated, were now sitting side by side, talking quietly.

At this point, he did not yet know if, in this tale of beer, whisky and weekly sex, there was also a dead body. What he did know more or less, because he had attended some in England, was how a coroner's inquest worked.

Quietly, almost timidly, Sergeant Ward had returned to his chair. Ezekiel was back wrestling with the ceiling fan and with an air of indifference, the coroner picked up where he had left off.

'The first time you stopped the car beyond the city limits was about eight miles out, just beyond the municipal airport. Why?'

Maigret could not follow, at first. Luckily, Ward's voice was so low that he was made to repeat his answer, and the big fellow's blush provided a clue.

'Latrine duty, sir.'

Perhaps he could not think of any other polite way of saying that they had had to pee.

'Everyone got out?'

'Yes, sir. I walked off, ten yards or so.'

'Alone?'

'No, sir. With him!'

Again he pointed out Mullins, against whom he seemed to hold a grudge.

'You don't know where Bessie went during this time?'

'I suppose she went off as well.'

It was hard not to think about the twenty beers they had each had.

'What time was it?'

'Between three and three thirty in the morning, I guess. I don't precisely know.'

'Did you see Bessie when you got back to the car?'

'No, sir.'

'And Mullins?'

'He showed up a few moments later.'

'From which direction?'

'I don't know.'

'What did you say to your friends?'

'I said, "To hell with her! That'll teach her a good lesson!"'

'Why?'

'Because that had already happened before.'

'What had happened before?'

'That she'd left me without any warning.'

'And you turned the car around?'

'Yes. I drove about a hundred yards back in the direction of Tucson, then stopped and got out again.'

'Why?'

'I figured she'd try to get back to the car and I wanted to give her a chance.'

'Was she drunk?'

'Yes, sir. But that had happened before, too. She still knew what she was doing.'

'Where did you go after leaving the car?'

'I walked towards the railway tracks that run parallel to the highway, about fifty yards away, in the desert.'

'Did you climb up on the tracks?'

'Yes, sir. I went about a hundred yards along it and must have stopped close to the place where Bessie had left us. I was calling her name.'

'Loudly?'

'Yes, but I didn't see her. She didn't answer. I thought she wanted to make me mad.'

'And you returned to your car. Didn't your friends say anything when they saw you start the engine and drive off to Tucson without bothering about her any more?'

'No, sir.'

'Do you consider this the act of a gentleman, abandoning a woman in the desert in the middle of the night?'

Ward made no reply. He had a low forehead, and Maigret was beginning to find that his heavy eyebrows gave him a mulish look.

'Did you go directly back to your base?'

Davis-Monthan, one of the main Air Force bases for B-29s, is about ten kilometres from Tucson, off in a different direction from the highway to Nogales.

'No, sir. I left three of my pals in town, near the bus station.'

'You kept one with you. Who?'

'Sergeant Mullins.'

'Why?'

'I wanted to look for Bessie.'

'You drove back along the highway?'

'Yes, sir. I stopped more or less where we parked the first time.'

'Did you go back to the railway tracks?'

A rather long silence.

'No. I don't believe so. I don't remember having got out of the car.'

'What did you do?'

'I don't know. I woke up at the wheel with the car turned towards Tucson, and there was a telegraph pole in front of me. I remember the pole and a nearby cactus.'

'Was Mullins still with you?'

'He was sleeping next to me, his chin on his chest.'

'So, as I understand it, you have no recollection of what happened before you woke up in front of the telegraph pole?'

When Ward's lips quivered, Maigret knew that he was about to say something important.

'No, sir. I had been drugged.'

'You mean to say that you weren't drunk?'

'I have often drunk as much as that and even more. I have never passed out. No one has ever drunk me into a stupor. I know my capacity. On that night, I'd been drugged.'

'According to you, someone might have put something in your drink?'

'Or in a cigarette. When I woke up, I reached automatically for my cigarettes in my pocket. I found Camels. Well, I only smoke Chesterfields. I was smoking a cigarette from that pack when I passed out – for the second time.'

'With Mullins right there.'

'Yes.'

'Do you suspect Mullins of having slipped some drugged cigarettes into your pocket?'

'Maybe.'

'Did you tell him so when you awakened?'

'No.'

'Did you speak to him?'

'No. I drove the car home. I live in town with my wife and children. Mullins came up to the apartment. I tossed him a pillow so that he could lie down on the couch. I went to sleep.'

'For how long?'

'I don't know. Perhaps an hour . . . At six a.m. I went to the base with him to go on duty and I got my aircraft in flying condition.'

'What does your job entail?'

'I'm a mechanic. I safety-check the aircraft before take-off and I remain on the airfield.'

'What did you do after that?'

'I left the base at around eleven that morning.'

'Alone?'

'With Dan Mullins.'

'When did you learn of the death of Bessie Mitchell?'

'At three that afternoon.'

'Where were you?'

'In a bar on Fifth Avenue. I was having a glass of beer with Mullins.'

'Had you drunk a lot of beer that morning?'

'Ten or twelve glasses. A sheriff came in and asked me if I was Sergeant Ward. I said I was, and he asked me to follow him.'

'You did not yet know that Bessie was dead?'

'I did not, sir.'

'You did not know that your three friends, whom you'd

left in front of the bus station, had taken a taxi back along the highway to Nogales as soon as you'd left them?'

'I did not, sir.'

'You didn't see the taxi along the way? You neither saw nor heard a train coming from Nogales?'

'No, sir.'

'At the base, that morning, you met none of those three friends?'

'I ran into Sergeant O'Neil.'

'He said nothing to you?'

'I don't remember his exact words. They were something like, "As for Bessie, that's all OK."'

'What did you make of that?'

'That she'd probably caught a ride home by hitch-hiking.'

'You didn't go to her place that day?'

'Yes, I did. When I left the base, at eleven. Erna told me that Bessie hadn't come home yet.'

'This was after Sergeant O'Neil told you that everything was OK?'

'Yes.'

'Did that not seem contradictory to you?'

'I thought that she had gone someplace else.'

'You did say earlier that you intended to obtain a divorce in order to marry Bessie.'

'Yes, sir.'

'You state positively that you did not see her again after you walked away from the car with Sergeant Mullins?'

'Not alive, no.'

'You saw her again when she was dead?'

'At the morgue, when the sheriff drove me there.'

'That first time you stopped, Sergeant Mullins was not in the car when you got back behind the wheel and he only reappeared a few moments later, correct?'

'Yes, sir.'

'Any questions, counsellor?'

The grey-haired attorney shook his head.

'Any questions, members of the jury?'

Same reaction from the five men and the pudgy woman who, anticipating what the coroner was about to say, was already getting out her knitting.

'Recess!'

Ezekiel lit his pipe, Maigret lit his. Everyone made a beeline for the arcade and rummaged through their pockets for nickels for the red Coca-Cola machine.

Some people, however, doubtless habitués, went through a mysterious door, and Maigret noticed when they reappeared that they had alcohol on their breaths.

Deep down, he was not yet too sure how real everything around him was. The old black juror with close-cropped hair and steel-framed glasses looked smilingly at him, as if they were already chums, and Maigret smiled back.

2. At the Head of the Class

Among the regular customers in a café, particularly out in the provinces, occasionally you see someone who has wandered in because he has an appointment, or a train to catch; sitting on a banquette, drowsy and bored, he keeps a vague eye on the card game in progress at the neighbouring table.

He is obviously unfamiliar with the game, but soon, intrigued, there he is, trying to figure it out. Little by little, he leans in to catch a glimpse of the cards in everybody's hands. Depending on the plays, now he is giving signs of approval or impatience, and the moment comes when it is all he can do to keep from intervening.

On that particular afternoon, Maigret saw himself as a little like that intruder in the provincial café, and this bothered him a bit. It was stronger than he was, though: he was hooked. He was in on the game. Already, during the interrogation of Sergeant Ward, he had been growing restless on his bench. There were questions the greenest of his inspectors would not have failed to ask but which had evidently never occurred to the little judge, so meticulous in his gestures and attire.

Of course, a coroner's inquest is not a trial. What the jurors had to decide was whether they thought Bessie Mitchell had died a natural death, an accidental death, or a death due to a malicious or criminal act.

The rest, in the case of those last two hypotheses, would come later, before a different jury.

'Tell us what happened on July 27, after seven thirty that evening.'

Wasn't it already rather naive to have allowed the four young men to hear their friend's testimony?

Sergeant O'Neil was smaller and stockier than the others. His light hair was wavy, slightly reddish. With his blunt features, he rather resembled a peasant from the north of France, a peasant well washed and polished to a shine.

Well washed they all were, along with almost everyone in the courtroom. These people had a look of health and cleanliness rarely seen in a European crowd.

'We went to the Penguin and did some drinking.'

This fellow was the good schoolboy, not necessarily the class brain, but the hardest worker. He looked up at the ceiling before answering, as if taking time to think in class, then replied slowly in an even, neutral voice while turning obediently towards the jury.

The four were boys, in a word, great big boys of twenty or more, well muscled and solidly built but boys all the same, whom you might casually have taken for grown-ups.

'How many glasses of beer did you have?'

'About twenty.'

'Who paid for the rounds?'

This one remembered. In time – because he took his own sweet time to reply – he announced that Sergeant Ward had paid for two rounds, while he, O'Neil, had bought only one, and that Dan Mullins had covered all the rest.

Maigret would have liked to have this witness all to himself in his office at Quai des Orfèvres and give him the third degree, just to see what he was made of.

One thing he would have asked him, among others (because aside from Ward, they were none of them married), was: 'Do you have a mistress?'

O'Neil's florid complexion suggested a person of hot-blooded sexual appetites. On the night in question there had been five of them for only one girl, and they were all, except for Wo Lee, rather drunk. In the darkness of the car, had not hands gone wandering?

The coroner was not considering such things, or, if he was, they went unmentioned.

'Who decided to go and end the night in Nogales?'

'I don't remember that exactly. I thought it was Ward.'

'You didn't hear Bessie suggest it?'

'No, sir.'

'Where were you all sitting in the car?'

It was as if he hadn't heard his comrade's testimony, he took such pains to remember.

'After a while, he had Bessie get in the back seat.'

'Why?'

'I guess he was jealous of Mullins.'

'Did he have any reason to be more jealous of Mullins than of the others?'

'I don't know.'

'What happened when the car got past the airport?'

'We pulled over.'

'For what reason?'

The witness studied the ceiling at even greater length,

hesitated, finally said – with a quick glance at Ward, who was staring at him, 'Because Bessie refused to go any farther.'

He seemed to be saying: 'I'm sorry, but it's the truth, and I swore to tell the whole truth.'

'Bessie didn't want to continue on to Nogales?'

'No, sir.'

'Why not?'

'I don't know.'

'What happened when you pulled over like that?'

There was the expression again, which had to be service lingo: latrine duty.

'Bessie went off on her own?'

The wait was even longer than the previous times, and his gaze stayed fixed on the ceiling.

'What I do remember is that when she came back, she was with Ward.'

'Bessie came back?'

'Yes, sir.'

'She got in the car again?'

'Yes. The car made a U-turn and took the highway back to Tucson.'

'At what moment did Bessie leave the car?'

'At the second stop. Right after the U-turn, Bessie told Ward she wanted to talk to him.'

'She was in the back, next to you?'

'Yes. Sergeant Ward stopped the car. They both got out.'

'In which direction did they go?'

'Over towards the railway tracks.'

'Were they gone a long time?'

'Sergeant Ward returned after twenty, twenty-five minutes.'

'You checked the time?'

'I didn't have a watch on.'

'He returned alone?'

'Yes. He said: "To hell with her! That'll teach her!"'

'What was he referring to?'

'That I don't know, sir.'

'You found it perfectly natural to return to town and abandon a woman in the desert?'

O'Neil did not reply.

'What did you talk about along the way?'

'We didn't talk.'

'Had you brought along anything to drink? Was there a bottle in the car?'

'I don't remember.'

'When Ward dropped you off in town, across from the bus station, did he tell you he was going back to look for Bessie?'

'No. He didn't say anything.'

'You weren't surprised that he didn't drive you back to the base?'

'I never thought about it.'

'What did you do then, you and Corporal Van Fleet and Wo Lee?'

'We took a taxi.'

'What did you talk about then?'

'Nothing.'

'Who had decided to take the taxi?'

'I don't know, sir.'

'How long was it between the moment when Ward and Mullins left you and when you took the taxi?'

'Three minutes, maybe . . . More like two.'

They really were stubborn children, who obviously had something to hide yet refused to give anything away. But why go about the interrogation in that fashion anyway? Maigret squirmed on his seat. He all but raised his hand to ask a question as if he, too, were still a schoolboy.

Suddenly spotting Harry Cole in the doorway, he blushed. How long had Cole been watching him with that satisfied smile? From the door his colleague made signs meaning: 'I suppose you'd prefer to stay?'

And in a little while, he went quietly away, leaving Maigret to his new passion.

'Where did the taxi drop you off?'

'At the place where we'd stopped the second time.'

'At the precise spot?'

'It was dark, so I can't say that. We did try to remember the exact spot.'

'What did you talk about on the drive out?'

'We didn't talk.'

'And you sent the taxi away? How did you plan on getting back to town and then out to the base?'

'By hitchhiking.'

'What time was it?'

'Around three thirty.'

'You didn't see Ward's car anywhere? You never saw either him or Dan Mullins?'

'No, sir.'

O'Neil avoided looking at Ward, whose gaze never left

him, and when their eyes did meet, the witness seemed to apologize, like a man obliged to do his duty.

'What did the three of you do, once you got out of the taxi?'

'We went in the direction of Nogales, then came back towards Tucson walking beside the railway tracks.'

'It never occurred to you to search for her on the other side of the highway?'

'No, sir.'

'Why not?'

'I don't know.'

'Did you walk for a long time?'

'Maybe an hour.'

'Without seeing anyone?'

'Yes, sir.'

'Without talking?'

'Yes, sir.'

'Then what happened?'

'We hailed a passing car that dropped us off at the base.'

'Can you tell me what make of car it was?'

'No, sir, but I believe it was a '46 Chevrolet.'

'Did you speak to the driver?'

'No, sir.'

'What did you do when you got back to the base?'

'We went off to bed. At six a.m. we got busy on our aircraft.'

Maigret was seething. He felt like shaking the little judge and saying: 'Haven't you ever grilled a witness in your life? Or are you avoiding all the vital questions on purpose?'

'When did you learn that Bessie Mitchell was dead?'

'When her brother told me about it, towards five that afternoon.'

'What precisely did he tell you?'

'That they'd found Bessie dead on the tracks, and there was going to be an inquest.'

'Who was present during that conversation?'

'Wo Lee was with me in the room. He said: "I know what happened." Mitchell began to question him. And Wo Lee just told him: "I'll talk only to the sheriff."'

It was just past five o'clock, and with the same abruptness as before the coroner adjourned the session by reciting offhandedly, while collecting the papers scattered across his desk, 'Tomorrow, nine thirty. Not here, but in Courtroom Two, one floor up.'

Everyone was leaving. The five Air Force men gathered outside under the arcade, still without exchanging a word, and an officer led them across the patio.

Waiting there in gaberdine trousers and a white shirt, Harry Cole looked like an athletic young man in a cheerful mood.

'Did you find that interesting, Julius? What would you say to a glass of beer?'

They went outside into instant heat and a thick glare where even sounds were deadened. The five or so tall buildings in Tucson stood out against the sky. People were driving off in their cars, even the Indian, who was opening the door of an old car with its bonnet tied down by twine. Maigret discovered that he had a wooden leg.

'I bet you have something to ask me, Julius . . .'

They were entering the cool interior of an air-conditioned

saloon where other gaberdine trousers and white shirts and bottles of beer were lined up all along the bar. There were also cowboys, real ones, with their high-heeled boots, broad-brimmed hats and blue jeans tight across their thighs.

'You're right. If we can postpone our visit to Nogales, I'd like to attend the next session of the inquest tomorrow.'

'Cheers! . . . No other questions?'

'Lots. I'll ask them as they come to mind. Are there any prostitutes around here?'

'Not in the sense you'd mean. In certain states in America, yes. They're illegal in Arizona.'

'Bessie Mitchell?'

'That's the replacement.'

'Erna Bolton as well?'

'More or less.'

'How many servicemen are on the base?'

'Five or six thousand . . . I've never thought about it.'

'Most are unmarried?'

'About three-quarters of them.'

'How do they manage?'

'The best they can. It's not that easy.'

His smile, which rarely left him, was genuine. He certainly respected, perhaps even rather admired Maigret, whom he knew by reputation. Still, it did amuse him to see a Frenchman wrestling with problems so completely foreign to him.

'Myself, I'm from the East,' he announced, not without a touch of pride. 'New England. Here, you see, it's still a little like frontier life. I could have you meet a few old-timers who shot it out with the Apaches at the turn of the

29

century and who sometimes formed an impromptu court to hang a horse or livestock rustler.'

Within the next half-hour they each had three bottles of beer, and Harry Cole reached a decision.

'Whisky time!'

Later on they drove off in the direction of Nogales; going through Tucson, Maigret was as disconcerted by the city as he had been in the courtroom. With a population of more than a hundred thousand, it was no small town.

And yet, outside the city centre and its business district with five or six twenty-storey buildings rising into the sky like towers, Tuscon looked like a house development

– or, rather, like a series of them one beside the other, some richer, others poorer, developments full of trim single-storey houses, all equally new.

Further along, streets were no longer paved. For great stretches there was nothing but sand and a few cacti. They drove past the airport, and suddenly the desert was everywhere, with the mountains violet in the distance.

'Here is about where it happened. Do you want to get out? Keep an eye open for rattlesnakes.'

'Are there any?'

'Sometimes they turn up even in the city.'

The railway tracks were a single line running about fifty metres from the highway.

'I think there are four or five trains every twenty-four hours. Sure you don't want to go and have a drink in Mexico? Nogales is right nearby.'

A hundred kilometres away! In the end, however, they drove there in less than an hour.

A small town with a fence cutting across the two main streets. Men in uniforms. Harry Cole spoke to them and a moment later he was plunging with Julius into a sudden bustle of people on narrow, littered streets bathed in a surprising bronze glow.

'We'll start at the Caves Bar, even though it is a mite too early.'

Half-naked urchins pestered them, eager to shine their shoes, and shopkeepers tried to detain them at the threshold of every souvenir store.

'As you can see, it's a carnival. When folks from Tucson or even Phoenix or farther away want to have fun, they come here.'

In the immense bar, they really did see nothing but Americans.

'You think Bessie Mitchell was killed?' asked Maigret.

'All I know is that she's dead.'

'Accidentally?'

'I have to say that it has nothing to do with me: it isn't a federal crime, and I deal only with them. Everything else is taken care of by the county police.'

In other words, the sheriff and his deputies. That was really what most bewildered Maigret, much more than the baroque and odorous funfair into which he had plunged.

In charge of the county police, the sheriff was in no way a public servant promoted through the ranks or by examinations, but a citizen elected much as a municipal councillor was in Paris. His previous occupation was of no importance. He put himself forward as a candidate and campaigned for the job.

Once elected, he chose his own deputies – his 'inspectors' – as he pleased: the fellows Maigret had seen with big revolvers and cartridge-studded belts.

'That's not all!' added Harry Cole with a touch of irony. 'Besides the appointed deputy sheriffs, there are all the others . . .'

'Like me?' joked Maigret, thinking of the silver badge he had received.

'I'm talking about the sheriff's friends, influential in his election, who get the same badge. For example, just about every rancher is a deputy sheriff. Don't think they take this lightly. A few weeks ago, a car stolen by a dangerous escaped convict was travelling between Tucson and Nogales. The sheriff of Tucson alerted a rancher who lives about halfway along that route and who then called two or three neighbours, livestock ranchers like himself. They were all deputy sheriffs. They set up a roadblock with their vehicles, and when the stolen car attempted to get past, they shot out its tyres, then made a show of firing at the driver, whom they wound up capturing with a lasso. What do you think of that?'

Maigret had not yet had as many drinks as the witnesses on the stand had put away, but it was beginning to tell on him, and he muttered with some difficulty, 'In France, the locals would have tried to stop the police instead.'

He was not sure exactly when they got back to Tucson . . .

Still in tow behind Cole, he had walked into the Penguin Bar towards midnight, although he was a little hazy on that point. There was a long counter of dark polished wood, with bottles of many colours on the shelves behind it. As in every bar, a soft light made the white shirts gleam.

In the place of honour at the back was a jukebox – imposing, big-bellied, chrome-plated – near a machine into which a middle-aged man fed coins for an hour, all in the hope of winning a free game by trying to drop small nickel-plated balls into holes.

Lit up on this pinball machine were naively drawn images of women in bathing suits. There was a completely naked woman in the style of *La Vie Parisienne* on a calendar over the bar.

Real women of flesh and blood, however, were hard to find. Only two or three sat at tables secluded by partitions about five feet high. These women were with companions. The couples sat motionless, hand in hand, before their glasses of beer and whisky, listening with vague smiles to the music streaming endlessly from the jukebox.

'Well, isn't this fun!' exclaimed Maigret with a grating laugh.

Cole irritated him, he could not have said why. Perhaps it was the man's unshakable self-confidence that rubbed him the wrong way.

He was a simple field agent of the FBI and he drove a big car with one hand, letting go of the wheel to light his cigarette at more than 100 kilometres an hour! He knew everyone. Everyone knew him. Whether he was here in the United States or in Mexico, he would tap people on the shoulder and they would turn around to exclaim affectionately: 'Hello, Harry!'

Cole would introduce Maigret, and they would shake his hand as if they had known him for ever, without wondering what he might be doing there.

'Have a drink!'

It didn't matter whether it was good or bad, as long as it was a drink. All along the counter here, men were stapled to their barstools and never moved except to lift a finger from time to time, a gesture the bartender knew by heart. A few Air Force non-coms were drinking along with the others. Perhaps the service had simple airmen, but Maigret had not yet seen one of them.

'If I understand correctly, they return to their base at any hour they please?'

Cole was surprised at his question.

'Of course!'

'At four in the morning, if they want?'

'As long as they're not on duty, they may even not show up at all.'

'And if they're drunk?'

'That's their business. What counts is that they do what they're assigned to do.'

Why did that infuriate him? Was it because he remembered his own military service and the ten o'clock curfew, those weeks of waiting for one wretched midnight pass?

'Don't forget, these men aren't conscripts.'

'I know. Where does the service recruit them?'

'Wherever they can. In the street. Haven't you seen the trucks that sometimes stop at a crossroads and play music? Inside there's a display of photographs of exotic countries, and a sergeant to explain the advantages of a military career.'

Cole always seemed to be playing with life, as if it were really quite amusing.

'You find all kinds in the armed services, it's the same everywhere. I suppose that where you come from, it isn't just the good little boys who sign up . . . Hello! Bill! My friend Julius . . . Have a drink!'

For the tenth or twentieth time that evening, Maigret heard a stranger tell him about his adventures in Paris. For all these fellows had been to Paris. All of them gave the same slightly ribald tone to their tales.

'Have a drink!'

If the coroner were to question him in the morning, he could answer like the others:

'I don't remember how many drinks. Maybe twenty?'

The more he drank, the more taciturn he became, to the point of looking as mulish as Sergeant O'Neil.

He had decided to understand, and he would understand. So there! He had already discovered why Harry Cole irritated him. The FBI man was convinced, in short, that Maigret was a big shot in his own country but that here, in the United States, he was incapable of figuring out anything. The more Cole watched him thinking things over, the more it amused him. Well, Maigret happened to believe that men and their passions are the same everywhere.

The important thing was to stop looking at differences, stop being astonished, for example, at the height of the buildings, at the desert, the cacti, the cowboys' hats and boots, the jukeboxes and machines for flipping little balls into holes.

'So: there were five servicemen and one girl,' he thought. 'And all but one of them had been drinking.'

They had been drinking the way Maigret was now drinking, mechanically, as all the men around him that evening were doing.

'Hello, Harry!'

'Hello, Jim!'

It was as if nobody there had a last name. And as if they were all the very best of friends. Each time Cole introduced someone to him, he would add meaningfully: 'A great guy!'

Or else: 'A fantastic fellow!'

Not once did he ever say: 'A bastard.'

Where were the bastards? Did this mean that there weren't any?

Or that standards were more forgiving here?

'Do you think that those five servicemen are free to go out tonight?'

'Why wouldn't they be?'

What he would have done with them in Paris! And above all, what they would have been in for when they returned to quarters!

'They haven't been charged with anything, have they?'

'Not yet,' grumbled Maigret.

'As long as a man has not been found guilty . . .'

'I know! I know!'

He drained his glass in an unpleasant humour. Then he considered one of the couples in their booth. Their lips had been locked together for a good five minutes, and the man's hands were nowhere to be seen.

'Tell me: they are probably not married, correct?'

'Correct.'

'So they have no right to go to a hotel?'

'Not unless they sign the register as man and wife, which is an offence that can cause them real trouble, especially if they have crossed state lines.'

'Where do they make love?'

'In the first place it's not certain that later on they'll still need to do so.'

Maigret shrugged angrily.

'And then there's the car.'

'And if they don't have one?'

'That's unlikely. Most people have a car. If they haven't, let them deal with it. It's their business, isn't it?'

'And if they're caught doing that in the street?'

'That will cost them a lot.'

'And if the girl is seventeen and a half instead of eighteen?'

'That can rack up around ten years in prison for her partner.'

'Bessie Mitchell wasn't eighteen . . .'

'But she'd been married and divorced.'

'Maggie Wallach, who seems to be the musician's mistress?'

'Why so?'

'It's obvious.'

'You've seen them at it?'

Maigret gritted his teeth.

'Mind you, she was married, too. And divorced.'

'And Erna Bolton, who's with the brother?'

'She's twenty.'

'You're familiar with the case?'

'Me? It has nothing to do with me. I already told you that there was no federal offence. If they had used the post office, for example, in the commission of a crime, that would fall under my jurisdiction. Or if they had smoked a single joint. Have a drink, Julius!'

There were twenty of them at the bar, drinking and staring straight ahead at the rows of bottles and the calendar showing a naked woman. There were naked – or half-naked – women just about everywhere, on the advertisements, the publicity calendars, and photos of pretty girls in bathing suits on every page of the newspapers and all the cinema screens.

'But good lord, what happens when these fellows want a woman?'

Harry Cole, more used to whisky than Maigret, looked him right in the eye and burst out laughing.

'They get married!'

The truth was, the coroner had been careful not to ask what seemed like the most basic questions. Was he hoping to arrive at the truth anyway? Did he simply not give a damn?

Perhaps, after all, the inquest was only a kind of formality, and no one was very eager to find out what had really happened that night.

One of the two men who had testified so far had lied, that was clear. It was either Sergeant Ward or Sergeant O'Neil.

Yet no one had seemed surprised by that. They were

both questioned with the same politeness, or, rather, the same detachment.

'Do you think they'll have the bartender testify?'

'What for?'

He was the same one serving them that evening, the one with a boxer's mug.

'They're going to throw us out,' announced Cole with a glance at the clock. 'Do you want anything to go?'

And seeing Maigret's amazement, he pointed out two of the customers.

'Look!'

At another counter off near the door, where bottles of spirits were sold, the men were buying flat pints that they slipped into their hip pockets.

'Maybe they've got a long road ahead of them, right? Or else they have some trouble sleeping.'

The FBI man was making fun of him, and Maigret did not say another word to him until he dropped him off in front of the Pioneer Hotel.

'I gather that you'll be spending the day tomorrow at the inquest?'

Maigret grunted a vague reply.

'I'll come get you at lunchtime. You're lucky: the proceedings will take place in Courtroom Two, upstairs, and it's air-conditioned. Good night, Julius!'

Without any malice, as if he were not talking about a dead girl, he added, 'Don't go dreaming about Bessie!'

3. The Little Chinese Fellow Who Did Not Drink

There were at least three people who said good morning to Maigret, and that pleased him. Like the first floor, the second floor of the county courthouse was surrounded by an arcade. The sun was already hot; groups of men waiting for Ezekiel's summons smoked cigarettes in the shade.

Ezekiel in particular, his big pipe in his mouth, nodded cordially at him, as did the juror with the wooden leg.

Maigret had been wondering, on the way over from his hotel, if the public's change of attitude towards Sergeant Ward would be noticeable.

On the previous day, when O'Neil was talking about the second time the car had stopped, his statement that Ward and Bessie had walked off together towards the railway tracks had been met, not with murmuring, but with something like a small collective shock. They must all have felt the same pang in their hearts.

Would they now look at Ward the way people instinctively do at those among them who have killed?

Not far from the officer who had brought them, the five airmen were there, smoking their cigarettes like everyone else, waiting to enter the courtroom. Like schoolboys who have fallen out with one another, they all kept at a certain distance.

It seemed to Maigret that Ward, his blue eyes lowering under big black brows, was standing more apart from the others, the object of distant furtive glances.

Had he gone home to sleep? What was his attitude towards his wife now? And hers towards him? Had he asked her to forgive him? Had they quarrelled to the point of separation?

The Chinese airman, with his big almond eyes, was as delicate and pretty as a girl.

He was short and seemed much younger than his friends. It's the same in school, where there is always one boy who is teased and called a sissy!

There were some new curious spectators. The newspaper had published its account of the first day under boldface headlines:

Sergeant Ward Claims He Was Drugged
O'Neil Contradicts His Testimony on Several Points

O'Neil still had the look of a conscientious prize student. Too conscientious. Had he and Ward conversed at all since the previous day?

Maigret had awakened in a bad mood, with a splitting headache and, to put it bluntly, a hangover, but that had passed. Still, it bothered him to have relied on the local remedy. Ever since his first days in New York, he'd been astonished to see people he had left seriously inebriated the night before turn up early the next morning bright-eyed and cheerful. After he'd been told the secret, he noticed in all the drugstores, cafés and bars those bottles of a particular blue mounted upside down on walls, with a nickel-plated spout that measured the proper dosage into a glass of water.

The water would begin to fizz and foam, and they would serve it to you as casually as if it had been a Coca-Cola or your breakfast coffee. A few minutes later, the lingering fumes of alcohol would be gone.

Why not? Next to the machines for getting drunk, the machine for getting sober. It was only logical.

'Members of the jury!'

They were going back into the classroom, and this one was more spacious than the previous day's venue. It looked like a real courtroom, with a balustrade between the court and the public like a communion rail, a desk for the coroner, a stand with a microphone for the witness. The jurors, seated in an authentic jury box, took on a new solemnity.

Now Maigret could better observe people he had not been able to see easily the day before, one of them a burly redhead who stayed close to the attorney, taking notes and speaking to him in a low voice. At first Maigret had taken him for a secretary or a journalist.

'Who's that?' he asked the man next to him.

'Mike!'

This he already knew; he'd heard others call him that.

'What does he do?'

'Mike O'Rourke? He's the chief deputy sheriff, the one in charge of the inquest.'

The county 'Maigret', in other words. They were both more or less equally large men, with the same spare tyre above their belts, the same thick necks, and they must have been the same age.

In the end, was it so different here from Paris? O'Rourke was not wearing his sheriff's badge or a revolver at his waist. He looked like a peaceable fellow, with a redhead's pale skin and eyes the colour of violets.

Was it the sheriff's idea? He often leaned down to whisper to the attorney. In any case, when the inquest began the attorney rose and asked for permission to question the last witness of the previous day. O'Neil was thus recalled to the stand, where the microphone was adjusted to his height.

'Did you notice the condition of the car in which you returned to the Tucson area? Wasn't it damaged?'

The good student frowned, looking up questioningly at the ceiling.

'I don't know.'

'Was it a two-door or a four-door model? Did you get in on the right or the left side?'

'I think it was a four-door. I got in on the side opposite the driver.'

'On the right-hand side, then. And you didn't notice any evidence that the car had been in an accident?'

'I don't remember any more.'

'You were quite drunk at the time?'

'Yes, sir.'

'More drunk than when Bessie left your group?'

'I don't know. Maybe.'

'And yet, you hadn't drunk anything after leaving the musician's house?'

'Correct, sir.'

'That's all.'

O'Neil stood up.

'Excuse me: one more question. Where were you sitting in that last car?'

'I was in front, next to the driver.'

The attorney indicated that he was through with the witness, and then it was Corporal Van Fleet's turn. He had fair, wavy hair and brick-red skin, and Maigret thought of him as 'the Dutchman'. Van Fleet's pals called him Pinky.

He was the first witness to seem nervous as he took his seat on the stand. He was making an obvious effort to appear calm but did not know where to look and even chewed his nails a few times.

'You're married? Single?'

'Single, sir.'

He had to cough to clear his throat, and the coroner slightly increased the volume of the microphone. He had an incredible armchair, that coroner. He could adjust it for various positions and spent his time leaning farther back, then a little forwards, then back again.

'Tell us what happened on July 27 after seven thirty that evening.'

A young black woman Maigret had noticed the previous day was sitting behind him, holding a baby, accompanied this time by her brother and sister. There were two pregnant women in the courtroom. Thanks to the air conditioning, it was quite cool, much cooler than the room downstairs, but Ezekiel kept fiddling importantly with this apparatus from time to time.

The Dutchman spoke slowly, with long silences during which he would search for words. The other four servicemen were all on the same bench with their backs to the visitors' gallery, and these comrades were the ones at whom Pinky glanced furtively, as if asking to be prompted.

The Penguin Bar, the musician's apartment, the departure for Nogales . . .

'Where were you sitting in Ward's car?'

'I started off in back with Sergeant O'Neil and Corporal Wo Lee, but I had to move up front when Ward told Bessie to change seats. There I sat on Mullins' right.'

'What happened then?'

'After passing the airport, the car stopped on the right-hand side of the highway, and we all got out.'

'Had you already decided not to continue on to Nogales?'

'No.'

'When did that come up?'

'When everyone had got back into the car.'

'Including Bessie?'

He hesitated, and Maigret felt that he was trying to catch a glimpse of O'Neil.

'Yes. Ward had announced that we were driving back to town.'

'It wasn't Bessie who told you that?'

'I heard Ward say it.'

'Did the car pull over a second time?'

'Yes. Bessie told Ward she wanted to talk to him.'

'Was she very drunk? Was she still aware of what she was doing?'

'I think so. They walked off together.'

'How long were they gone?'

'Ward came back, alone, after about five or six minutes.'

'That's what you're saying, five or six minutes? Did you check the time?'

'No. But I don't think he was gone longer than that.'

'And then what did he say?'

'He didn't say anything.'

'Didn't anyone ask him what had happened to Bessie?'

'No, sir.'

'Weren't you surprised to be leaving without her?'

'A little, maybe.'

'The whole trip back, Ward said nothing more about it?'

'No, sir.'

'Who decided to take a taxi to go back to that spot?'

Van Fleet gestured towards O'Neil.

'Didn't the two of you discuss whether or not to take Wo Lee along with you?'

Maigret, who looked as if he were dozing, gave a start. Again, a seemingly innocuous question appeared to suggest that the coroner knew more than he wanted to let on. O'Rourke, moreover, was just then hovering at the ear of the attorney, who was writing something down.

'No, sir.'

'What did you talk about during the ride?'

'We didn't talk.'

'When the taxi stopped, didn't you and O'Neil discuss anything?'

'I don't remember. No, sir.'

O'Rourke must have been good at his job. Without

much effort he had located the taxi-driver, whom they would doubtless see later testifying in turn.

Of the three servicemen questioned so far, Pinky had been the most ill at ease.

'Don't you sleep in the same room as O'Neil? How long have you been roommates?'

'About six months.'

'Are you close friends?'

'We always go out together.'

When the attorney was asked if he had any questions for the witness, he had only one.

'Was the car in which you returned to the base in good condition?'

Pinky could not answer that particular question, either. He had not noticed the make of the car. He remembered only that it had been white or light-coloured.

'Recess!'

It was strange: for no apparent reason, Sergeant Ward was already looking less like a murderer. It was O'Neil, now, whom people considered as they went by. Perhaps he was perfectly innocent. Perhaps they all were. And they felt suspicion shifting from one to another of them. Perhaps they were even suspecting one another? What were they thinking, smoking their cigarettes outside and drinking their Coca-Colas?

Although Maigret could have introduced himself to Mike O'Rourke, who would have clapped him on the shoulder and probably enlightened him on vital points, he found it more entertaining to watch the comings and goings of his colleague, who took advantage of the temporary recess to make a few telephone calls from a glassed-in office.

When the inquest was about to resume, the attorney wound up missing and had to be sought throughout the building. Perhaps he'd had some phone calls to make as well?

'Corporal Wo Lee.'

He slipped into his seat on the stand; the microphone was positioned in front of his mouth. He spoke so softly that it was difficult to hear him even with amplification.

The three previous witnesses had already taken their time with each answer. As for Wo Lee, he paused for so long that he seemed to have gone blank or have suddenly started thinking about something else.

Were they, like a band of schoolboys who had been up to mischief, accusing one another of snitching?

Maigret had to lean forwards and listen closely, because Wo Lee was hard to follow.

'Tell us what happened on the . . .'

His testimony was so slow that before they reached the departure for Nogales the coroner announced another recess. Three prisoners in blue uniforms were brought before him during the hiatus, men whom the police had arrested the day before and who had nothing to do with the current case.

A Mexican with strong Indian features was accused of drunkenness and disturbance of the peace on the public thoroughfare.

'Do you plead guilty?'

'Yes.'

'Five dollars or five days. Next!'

A bounced cheque.

'You plead guilty? We'll schedule your hearing for August 7. Bail is set at five hundred dollars.'

Maigret went downstairs for a Coca-Cola, and two of the jurors gave him a smile as he went by. When he had to cross a patch of sunshine, he felt it burning his skin.

When he returned, Wo Lee was already on the stand, answering a question that had just been put to him. Now there were people standing in front of the open door, but Maigret was pleased to see that no one had taken his empty seat.

'Just when we were leaving the bar,' Wo Lee was saying slowly, 'we bought two bottles of whisky.'

'What happened at the musician's place?'

'Bessie and Sergeant Mullins went into the kitchen. A bit later, Sergeant Ward went there too, and there was an argument.'

'Between the two men, or between Ward and Bessie?'

'I don't know. Ward came back holding a bottle.'

'Had both bottles been drunk?'

'No. One had been left in the car.'

'On the front or the back seat?'

'On the back seat.'

'On which side?'

'On the left side.'

'Who sat on the left side?'

'Sergeant O'Neil.'

'Did you observe him drinking during the drive?'

'It was too dark for me to see him.'

'During the evening, did Harold Mitchell seem angry at his sister?'

'No, sir.'

Bessie's brother, by the way, was now in uniform. In civvies the day before, wearing a shirt of a nasty violet, he had looked like the classic bad boy in films.

Wearing clean, crisply pressed cotton duck trousers, he seemed more respectable. At one point during Wo Lee's testimony, the musician, who had been outside, came to get Mitchell and murmured briefly to him out in the arcade. When Mitchell returned, he went over to Mike O'Rourke, who then spoke to the attorney, who in turn rose to address the bench.

'Sergeant Mitchell requests that a witness be called as soon as possible.'

Sergeant Mitchell had sat down where he had been the day before, next to Maigret. When the coroner turned towards him he rose to speak in a quavering voice.

'There's been talk that certain men on the train noticed a piece of rope around my sister's wrist. I'd like them to testify here.'

At a signal he sat down again; the coroner spoke to his bailiff, then resumed his interrogation.

'What happened when the car pulled over about a mile past the airport?'

Once more, in a different accent, the words 'latrine duty' automatically brought a smile to people's lips, as if the term had become a running gag.

'Did you see Bessie walk away from the car?'

'Yes. She went off with Sergeant Mullins.'

Now it was his back everyone stared at, and Ward seemed less and less like a murderer.

'Were they gone a long time? Where was Ward during this period?'

'He was one of the first to return to the car. Then Bessie got in as well, and we had to wait a few minutes for Mullins.'

'How long were Bessie and Mullins together?'

'Maybe ten minutes.'

'Had it already been decided not to continue on to Nogales?'

'No. It was when we were setting out again that Bessie said she'd had enough and wanted to go home.'

'Did Ward turn around without any argument?'

'Yes, sir.'

'Tell us what happened next. You had nothing to drink all that evening, correct?'

'Only Coca-Cola. After a hundred yards, Bessie asked him to pull over again.'

'Did she say anything else?'

'No.'

'Who got out of the car with her?'

'No one, at first. She walked off on her own. Then Dan Mullins got out.'

'You're sure it was Mullins?'

'Yes, sir.'

'Was he gone a long time?'

'At least ten minutes. Maybe more.'

'Did he head for the railway tracks?'

'Yes. Then Sergeant Ward got out, on the left side, and

walked all around the car. He came back almost immediately because we could hear Mullins' footsteps.'

'Did the two men exchange words?'

'No. We drove off. Sergeant O'Neil, Van Fleet and I, we got out in front of the bus station.'

'Who suggested going back out on the highway?'

'Sergeant O'Neil.'

'Were you asked not to go along with them?'

'Not exactly. O'Neil just wondered if I wasn't too tired and wouldn't rather return to the base.'

'What was said in the taxi?'

'Van Fleet and O'Neil talked quietly. I was in front with the driver and didn't listen.'

'Who showed the driver where to stop?'

'O'Neil.'

'Was it the first or the second spot where the car had pulled over?'

'I can't say. It was still dark.'

'Wasn't there some kind of discussion at that time?'

'No, sir.'

'Wasn't there any talk about perhaps having the taxi wait?'

'No, sir.'

They had not discussed that. They had come to look for the girl abandoned in the desert and they were not keeping the taxi to take her back to town.

'You never encountered or passed other cars along the highway?'

'No, sir.'

'What did you do after the taxi left?'

'We walked towards Nogales and then, after about a mile, we turned around.'

'Together?'

'Going out, yes. Coming back, I walked along the edge of the highway. Sergeant O'Neil and Pinky were farther out in the desert.'

'On the side with the railway tracks?'

'Yes, sir.'

'How long did all this walking take?'

'About an hour.'

'And for an hour, you saw no one? None of you heard any train? What colour was the car that brought you back to town?'

'A light yellow.'

The attorney rose once more to ask the ritual question he found so mysteriously important.

'Did you notice whether the car showed any traces of a recent accident?'

'No, sir. I got in on the right-hand side.'

'And O'Neil?'

'He did, too. It was a sedan. He got in the front seat, and I was in the back. Pinky walked around to the other side.'

'Was the bottle of whisky still with you?'

'No.'

'Was it in the taxi?'

'I'm not sure. I don't believe so.'

'The following day, when Harold Mitchell told you that his sister had been killed, you said you knew what had happened, but that you'd speak only in the presence of the sheriff.'

Maigret saw Mitchell's hand grip his knee hard.

'No, sir.'

'Didn't you speak to him?'

'I told him: "The sheriff will question us, and I'll tell him what I know."'

That was obviously not the same thing, and next to Maigret Mitchell gestured nervously in anger and chagrin.

Was Wo Lee lying? Out of the four witnesses heard so far, who was lying?

'Recess! The hearing will continue downstairs, in the justice of the peace's room, at one thirty.'

Harry Cole had promised to be there but was not, and Maigret caught sight of him a little later, getting out of his car across from the county courthouse. He was as fresh-faced and alert as he had been the previous day, with the same seemingly inexhaustible good humour. It was the serene cheerfulness of a man who has no nightmares, who feels at peace with himself and everyone else.

They were almost all of them like that, and it definitely got Maigret's back up.

It made him think of clothing that was too neat, too clean, too well pressed. It was like their houses, as immaculate as clinics, so impersonal that there was no particular reason to sit in one place rather than another.

Basically, he suspected them of harbouring the anxieties every human being feels and of adopting this light-hearted façade out of a sense of propriety.

Even the five airmen, in his opinion, were not showing

the proper concern. Each remained locked inside himself, yet you never sensed the uneasiness of people who, rightly or wrongly, are suspected of a crime.

The spectators seemed completely unaffected. No one, apparently, spared a thought for the girl who had died on the railway tracks. It was more like a kind of game, and only the reporter from the *Star* saw fit to add some sensational headlines.

'Did you sleep well, Julius?'

If only they would stop calling him that! The worst part was that they weren't doing it on purpose, they meant no harm at all.

'Have you solved the problem? Is it a crime, a suicide, or an accident?'

Entering the bar on the street corner as if it were home, Maigret recognized several spectators, including two jurors.

'Have a drink! You had a case rather like this in France, didn't you? A judge found dead on some railway tracks. What was his name again?'

'Prince!' grumbled Maigret testily.

And that struck him, because in that case as well there had been some rope found around the man's wrists.

'How did it end?'

'It hasn't.'

'Do you have your own idea about that?'

He did, but he preferred not to mention it, because his opinion on the subject had brought him enough trouble, along with attacks from certain quarters of the press.

'Did you have a chat with Mike? You've met him, haven't

you? He's the chief deputy sheriff and takes personal charge of important cases. Do you want me to introduce you?'

'Not yet.'

'In that case, let's go have some steak and onions, and I'll drop you off at the courthouse when it's time.'

'You're not following the case at all?'

'I told you, it has nothing to do with me.'

'And it doesn't interest you, either?'

'One can't take an interest in everything, right? If I do Mike O'Rourke's job, who'll do mine? Tomorrow or the next day, maybe, I'm going to finally get my hands on $20,000 worth of drugs that turned up around here a week ago.'

'How did you find that out?'

'Through our agents in Mexico. I even know who sold the shipment, for how much, on what day. I know when it crossed the border at Nogales. I think I know what truck brought it to Tucson, too. After that, I'm just guessing.'

The waitress at the cafeteria, a buxom blonde of about twenty, was pretty and blooming with youth.

'Hello, Doll!' Cole called out to her.

And added to Maigret: 'She's a student at the university. She's hoping to get a scholarship to go and finish her studies in Paris.'

Why did Maigret feel the need to be vulgar?

What was this mood that came over him whenever he found himself with Harry Cole?

'What if someone pinched her derrière?' he asked, thinking of the waitresses in the little bistros of France.

56

His colleague seemed surprised and gave him a long look, as if seriously considering his question.

'I don't know,' he finally admitted. 'Maybe you could give it a try? Doll!'

Did he really expect Maigret to reach out while the young woman leaned over them, her white uniform taut over her firm flesh?

'Sergeant Mullins!'

Another bachelor. The only one of the airmen who was married and had children was Ward.

Wasn't it Dan Mullins, now, who appeared to be the villain?

'Tell us what happened on the night of the . . .'

Maigret preferred the smaller room to the one upstairs, even though this one was hotter. It was cosier. And Ezekiel, who felt more at home here, was much more picturesque.

He was the exam monitor. The coroner was the teacher, and the attorney, a school inspector.

Perhaps they were going to decide at last to ask the essential questions? Sergeant Ward had admitted that he was jealous of his friend Mullins, the one he had found with Bessie in the musician's kitchen.

Well, once again, it was not to be.

Five men and one girl had spent the better part of a night together. All, except for Wo Lee, had been keyed up by their drinking. Four of the five men were single, and Maigret now knew how limited their options were for sexual satisfaction. As for Ward, who was the possessive type, he seemed to have had Bessie under his skin.

Not one word! Still the same old questions, which the coroner himself seemed to find so unimportant that he asked them while gazing elsewhere, at the ceiling, mostly. Was he even listening to the replies?

Only Mike O'Rourke, the county's Maigret, was taking notes and showing interest in the case. Seated behind Maigret, the black woman breast-fed her baby. A little girl and a fat woman, both black, had joined her entourage. If the inquest went on for a long time, the whole tribe would fill up the courtroom.

'Had you met Bessie before?'

'Once, sir.'

'Alone?'

'I was with Ward when he met her for the first time, at the drive-in. I left them when they went off in the car at around three in the morning.'

'Did you know that Sergeant Ward intended to get a divorce in order to marry her?'

'No, sir.'

That was the end of that line of questioning.

'What happened when the car pulled over a little way past the airport?'

'We all got out. I went off by myself for latrine –'

– duty: that much they all knew! It was becoming an obsessive image, those five men and one girl, scattered around the car, expelling all the liquid they had imbibed that night.

'You went off on your own?'

'Yes, sir.'

'Did you see Sergeant Ward?'

'I saw him disappear into the darkness with Bessie.'

'Did they return together?'

'Ward came back and got behind the wheel. Then he said impatiently: "To hell with her! That'll teach her."'

'Pardon me: was it during the first stop that Ward said that?'

'Yes, sir. There was no other stop before Tucson.'

'Didn't Bessie ask Ward to follow her, on the pretext that she wanted to talk to him?'

'Before, yes.'

'Before what?'

'Right when the car pulled over. She was the one who told him that she didn't want to go any farther, and Ward slowed down. Then she added, "I need to talk to you. Come on."'

'At the first stop?'

'There was no other stop.'

The silence was rather long. Seen from the back, the four servicemen never moved.

'Then what?' sighed the coroner.

'We went back to town and we dropped off the three others.'

'Why did you stay with Ward?'

'Because he asked me to.'

'When?'

'I don't remember.'

'Did he tell you he meant to go and look for Bessie?'

'No, but that's what I understood.'

'Did you give him any cigarettes?'

'No. Along the way, he asked me to get his pack from his pocket. I took a cigarette from it and lit it for him.'

'Was it a Chesterfield?'

'No, sir. A Camel. There were three or four left in the pack.'

'Did you smoke any of them, too?'

'I don't think so. I don't remember. I fell asleep.'

'Before the car stopped?'

'I believe so, or else right after. When Ward woke me up, I saw a telegraph pole and a cactus near the car.'

'Neither of you got out of the car?'

'I don't know if Ward got out. I was sleeping. He took me to his place and tossed me a pillow so I could bed down on the couch.'

'Did you see his wife?'

'Not that time. I heard them talking.'

'In short, you both drove back along the highway to look for Bessie, and neither of you got out of the car.'

'Yes, sir.'

'Did you see any other cars? Did you hear the train?'

'No, sir.'

All those hale and hearty fellows were between eighteen and twenty-three years old. Bessie, who was seventeen, had already been married, divorced and – now – was dead.

'Recess!'

Walking past a glassed-in office, Maigret heard the attorney talking on the phone.

'Yes, doctor. In a few minutes. Thank you. We'll wait . . .'

It was probably the doctor who had performed the

autopsy and who would be the next witness. He must have been quite busy, for the break went on for more than half an hour, giving the coroner time to work his way through five or six ordinary offenders.

The officer who had escorted the five airmen was called over for consultation by the attorney and Mike O'Rourke, who were having an animated discussion in a corner of the corridor. Shortly thereafter they closeted themselves in the office marked 'private', where the coroner then joined them.

4. The Man Who Wound Clocks

One of Maigret's uncles, his mother's brother, had one mania. As soon as he entered a room with a clock in it – no matter what kind of clock, large or small, an old pendulum clock with a glass-fronted case or an alarm-clock on the mantelpiece – he was unable to attend to any conversation until he could at last go over to wind up the timepiece.

He did this everywhere, even when visiting people whom he hardly knew. Sometimes he did the same thing in a shop where he had gone to purchase a pencil or some nails.

He was not a clockmaker, however: he worked in the Registry Office.

Did Maigret take after his obsessive uncle in some way? Cole had left him a note at the hotel reception desk, with a flat key in the envelope.

Dear Julius,
    Have to make a quick hop to Mexico by plane. Probably back tomorrow morning. My car in the hotel parking lot. Key enclosed.
    Sincerely yours.

What would Cole have thought of him, of the French police, if he had known that Maigret had never learned to drive?

In these parts, men his age flew private planes. Most ranchers, who were really only large-scale farmers, had their own planes, which they employed to go fishing on Sundays. And many even used helicopters to crop-dust their fields.

Maigret had not felt like eating alone in the hotel dining room and had set off on foot. He had been wanting for some time to roam the streets but had never been given the chance. To go two blocks, people jumped into their cars.

He passed a handsome white-colonnaded building in the colonial style surrounded by a well-kept lawn. The previous evening, he had noticed the glowing neon sign of the Caroon Mortuary, a local funeral home.

'The Best Funeral at the Best Price', said their newspaper advertisement.

And every evening, the undertaker sponsored a half-hour of soothing music on the radio. It was Dr Caroon who did the embalming. Maigret had received frankly disgusted looks after announcing that in France they put dead people in the ground without gutting them like chicken or fish.

The wiry, nervous little doctor had seemed quite hurried and hadn't said much at the inquest. He had mentioned the head ('completely scalped'), two severed arms, flesh 'brought to me higgledy-piggledy'.

'Can you determine the cause of death?'

'It was definitely caused by the impact of the locomotive. The top of the skull was torn off like the lid from a box, and bits of brain tissue were found several yards away.'

'Do you affirm that Bessie was still alive at the moment of impact?'

'Yes, sir.'

'Could she not have been unconscious, from the effects of either blows or intoxication?'

'That is possible.'

'Did you find any traces of blows that might have been delivered before her death?'

'Given the state of the body, such a determination is impossible.'

That was all. No mention of any examinations of a more intimate order that might have been made.

Maigret was almost alone as he walked along downtown, and it had been like that in every American city he had visited. No one lives in the heart of the city. As soon as the offices and stores close, the crowd streams back towards the residential neighbourhoods, leaving almost-empty streets where the shop windows, however, stay lit up all night long.

He came to a drive-in eatery and suddenly felt a craving for a hot dog. Half a dozen parked cars were fanned out in front of the door, and two girl carhops were serving their occupants. There was in fact a kind of counter inside, with stools anchored to the floor, but somehow Maigret felt shabby at the idea of arriving on foot and sitting inside.

He felt it several times a day, this impression of shabbiness. These people had everything. In no matter what small town, the cars were as numerous and luxurious as on the Champs-Élysées. Everyone wore new clothes, new shoes; shoe repair shops were hard to find. Crowds all looked well scrubbed and prosperous.

The houses were new, too, full of the latest appliances. They had everything: that was the right word.

Yet five young fellows in their twenties were up before the coroner because they'd spent the night drinking with a girl who had then been torn apart by a train.

Why should it matter to him? He was not here to worry about that. Study tours like this one he had been offered after so many years were more like pleasure trips. He had only to allow himself to be escorted from city to city, accepting fine dinners, whiskies and cocktails, deputy-sheriff badges, listening to the stories he was told.

He couldn't help it: he was as anxious as he was in France whenever he plunged into a complicated case he had to resolve at all costs.

They had everything: fine. And yet the newspapers were filled with accounts of crimes of every kind. In Phoenix the authorities had just arrested a gang of violent offenders, the oldest of whom was fifteen and the youngest, twelve. Only yesterday, an eighteen-year-old student in Texas had killed his wife's sister – since he already had a wife. A thirteen-year-old girl, already married as well, had just given birth to twins while her husband was in prison for robbery.

Maigret headed automatically for the Penguin Bar. Going there by car had made the trip a breeze. Now he had a better idea of how big the city was and he began to regret not having taken a taxi, as he was streaming with perspiration.

They had everything. So why had the people at the Penguin the previous evening been so dejected?

Was Maigret taking after his uncle who wound up clocks, even some that weren't his? He had never thought about the man that way and perhaps he was discovering the real reason for his uncle's mania: he must have had a phobia about run-down clocks. Well, a ticking clock can stop from one moment to another. People are careless, forget to wind up the mechanism.

It was instinctive: his uncle did it for them.

Maigret as well felt uneasy when he sensed that something was out of kilter. So he would try to understand, stick his nose in everywhere, sniffing around.

What was out of kilter in this country, where they had everything?

The men were tall and strong, healthy, well groomed and in general, rather cheerful. The women were almost all pretty. The stores were bursting with merchandise, the houses were the most comfortable in the world, there were cinemas on every street corner, no beggars to be seen and poverty seemed unknown.

The undertaker paid for a music programme on the radio, and cemeteries were delightful parks that people felt no need to surround with walls and iron railings as if they feared the dead. The houses as well had green lawns, and at that hour men in shirtsleeves or no shirts at all were watering their flowers and grass. There were no fences or hedges to shut the gardens off one from another.

Dear God, they had everything! They organized themselves scientifically to make life as pleasant as possible and from the moment the alarm went off, your radio would affectionately wish you a good day on behalf of some brand of hot cereal, without forgetting your birthday when the time came.

So, what was it?

That question was doubtless why Maigret was becoming so interested in those five men whom he didn't know from Adam or Eve, and in Bessie who was dead and whom he'd never seen even in a photo, and in the other people who paraded through the courtroom.

Many things vary from one country to another. Others are the same everywhere.

But what changes colour the most across borders? Might it be poverty?

Maigret was familiar with the poverty of the poor neighbourhoods of Paris, of the little bistros of Porte d'Italie or Saint-Ouen, the filthy destitution of the slums outside Paris and the discreet penury of Montmartre and Père-Lachaise. The rock-bottom misery of the river embankments, of Place Maubert or the Salvation Army.

That kind of poverty you could understand, and trace its origins, follow its development.

The poverty he sensed here was not unwashed and in rags, it was poverty with bathrooms, and it seemed harsher to him, more desperate, more pitiless.

Finally, he pushed open the door to the Penguin and hoisted himself on to a barstool. The barman remembered him and what he'd had the previous evening.

'Manhattan?' he asked cordially.

Maigret said yes. It was all the same to him. It was only

eight in the evening. Night had not yet fallen, but there were already twenty or so customers bellied up to the bar, while certain tables in the booths were occupied.

A girl wearing slacks and a white blouse was waiting on people in the bar. He had not noticed her the previous evening. He watched her. Her slacks, of a thin black gaberdine, clung to her hips and thighs with every step. She seemed to have stepped out of a billboard, a calendar, a cinema magazine.

When she had finished serving, she slipped a nickel into the jukebox and selected a sentimental tune. Then she sat with her elbows on one corner of the bar, dreaming.

There were no terraces where people could have an aperitif, watch passers-by in the setting sun and breathe the scent of chestnut trees.

They drank, but to do so had to shut themselves up inside bars sealed off from the eyes of others, as if satisfying some shameful need.

Was that why they drank more?

The engine driver had been questioned last. He was a middle-aged, well-dressed man whom Maigret had initially taken for a civil servant.

'When I first saw the body, it was too late to stop my train because I had sixty-eight loaded freight cars behind me.'

Fruits and vegetables from Mexico in refrigerated cars: such things came in from every country of the world. Hundreds of ships arrived in the ports every day.

They had simply everything.

'Was it day yet?'

'It was beginning to get light. She was lying across the tracks.'

They had brought him a blackboard. He had drawn two chalk lines for the tracks and, between them, had sketched a kind of marionette.

'This is the head.'

Neither her head nor any of her limbs touched the rails.

'She was on her back, her knees up, like this. Here, this is an arm. There's the other, which was torn off.'

Maigret looked at the shoulders of the five servicemen, especially Ward's. Perhaps he had loved Bessie. Had Ward, or one of his friends, made love to her that night?

'The body was dragged over a distance of about thirty yards.'

'Did you have time to see, before the impact, whether she was alive?'

'That I can't say, sir.'

'Did you have the impression that her wrists were tied?'

'No, sir. As you can see on the drawing, her hands were clasped over her stomach.'

And in a low voice, he added hurriedly, 'I was the one who collected the pieces along the tracks.'

'Is it true that you found some string?'

'Yes, sir. It was just a small thing, about six inches long. You find all kinds of stuff on the tracks.'

'Was the string near the body?'

'Maybe a yard away.'

'You didn't find anything else?'

'Actually, I did, sir.'

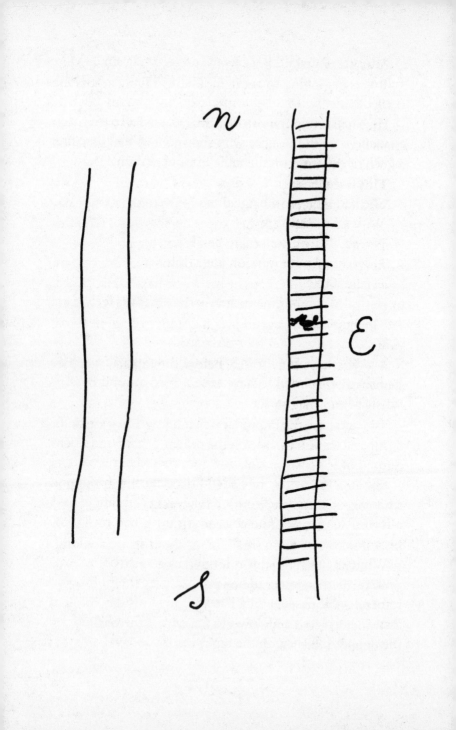

After searching his pockets, he pulled out a small white button.

'It's a shirt button. I automatically put it in my pocket.'

He handed it to the coroner, who passed it to the attorney, and it was O'Rourke who showed it to the jury, after which he placed it on the table in front of him.

'How was Bessie dressed?'

'She was wearing a beige dress.'

'With white buttons?'

'No, sir. The buttons were beige, too.'

'How many men were on your train?'

'Five in all.'

Harold Mitchell, the brother, had risen to his feet again. He was allowed to speak.

'I ask that the other four be heard.'

It was the engine driver's assistant, he explained, who had seen or claimed to have seen a cord around Bessie's wrists before the impact.

'Recess!'

Something had happened, however, that Maigret had not really understood. At one point, the attorney had stood up and spoken to the coroner, but Maigret had caught only a few of his words. The coroner, in turn, had reeled off his adjournment.

While everyone else was leaving the courtroom, however, the five servicemen had not followed their officer to return to the base as they had the previous day but had instead been escorted down to the end of the corridor by the deputy sheriff with the big revolver.

Maigret had been curious enough to go and take a look. He'd found a thick iron door, bars, and, behind them, other bars, those of the jail cells.

Out under the colonnade, he had approached one of the jurors.

'They were arrested?'

Because of his accent, the man did not understand him right away.

'For having contributed to the delinquency of a minor, yes.'

'Wo Lee as well?'

'He bought one of the bottles!'

So they were locked up for having made Bessie drink, Bessie who at seventeen had been married, divorced and was more or less involved in prostitution.

Maigret was aware that when travelling, a man is always a little ridiculous, because he would would like life to go on just as it does back home.

Maybe these people had their own approach to the problem? Maybe this coroner's inquest was only a formality and the real investigation was going on elsewhere?

He had the proof of it that evening. When one of the regulars lumbered off after calling out a general goodnight to the crowd, Maigret noticed O'Rourke, who had been hidden by the other man.

He was sitting in one of the booths, with a bottle of beer in front of him. The waitress had come over and sat down beside him. They seemed like good friends. The chief deputy sheriff was talking to the girl, stroking her arm, and had offered her a drink.

Did he know Maigret by sight? Had Harry Cole pointed him out among the spectators at the inquest?

Maigret was pleased to see his American colleague in the bar. Hadn't that always been his own habit? This was doubtless not O'Rourke's first visit to the Penguin. He wasn't playing the cop. He was slumped off in his corner. He was smoking cigarettes, not a pipe. And he did something rather surprising. At one point, he lit a cigarette and, quite casually, after taking a few puffs, he held it out to the girl, who put it between her lips.

Had she been here the night of Bessie's death? Probably. She must be here every evening. She had served them.

O'Rourke was saying something funny, and she was laughing. She had served a couple who had just walked in, then returned to sit by him.

He seemed to be flirting with her. He had red hair in a crew cut and a ruddy complexion.

Why didn't Maigret go and sit near them? All he had to do was introduce himself.

'*Un demi!*' he said.

Startled, he caught himself right away: 'A beer!'

The beer was strong, like an English brew. Many patrons ignored their glasses to drink straight from the bottle. Next to Maigret was a cigarette machine like the vending machines for chocolates in the Paris Métro.

What was out of kilter?

In talking with him about armed forces recruitment, Harry Cole had said, 'Among others, we get lots of folks on parole.'

Maigret had not understood, so Cole had gone into detail.

'Here, when a man is sentenced to two years, five years in prison or even more, it doesn't mean that he spends his complete sentence in the penitentiary. If his conduct is satisfactory, after a certain time, maybe a few months, he is released on parole. He's free, but must give an account of himself to a police officer, every day at first, then every week, finally every month.'

'Do many of them fall back into crime?'

'I don't have any statistics to hand. The FBI complains that parole is given too easily. Some folks on parole commit theft or murder barely a few hours after their release. Others prefer to join the armed services, which automatically releases them from police surveillance.'

'Was this the case with Ward?'

'I don't believe so. Mullins, I think, has been sentenced several times for minor offences. Especially for assault and battery. He's from Michigan. Those guys are tough.'

Another thing that baffled Maigret was that people were almost never from the place where they were. Here in Tucson, the coroner – who doubled as the justice of the peace – was from Maryland, but had gone to college in California. The engine driver who had testified earlier was from Tennessee. And the barman at the Penguin must have come straight from Brooklyn.

Up in the big cities of the North, there were slums, impoverished areas with apartment buildings like barracks, where men were hardened by life and the street kids quickly formed neighbourhood gangs.

In the South, the people outside the cities lived in wooden shacks surrounded by rubbish.

But this was not an explanation, Maigret realized that. There was something else, and he drank his beer while staring stubbornly over at his colleague and the waitress.

For an instant he wondered if O'Rourke were really there to keep an eye on him. It was not impossible. In spite of his air of taking life and other people lightly, Harry Cole might well have guessed that he would come to the Penguin that evening. Perhaps someone wasn't pleased to see him nosing around the case?

He was wrong to drink too much. But what else was there to do? He couldn't sit outside for an hour with his glass, as on a terrace. Neither could he wander alone on foot down endless streets. He didn't feel like going to a cinema or shutting himself up in his hotel room.

He was doing what the others all did. When his glass was empty, he signalled to the barman, who refilled it, and he told himself that in the morning he would simply turn to that blue drugstore bottle to get back on his feet.

He had written down the address where Bessie had lived with Erna Bolton. In the end he slid off his bar-stool and walked up and down the neighbourhood trying to decipher the names or, rather, the numbers of the streets.

As soon as you left the commercial artery with its shining shop windows, the streets grew dark, with houses separated from one another by lawns.

Did people leave their shutters and curtains open on purpose?

All the houses had front porches and on almost all of them you saw families relaxing in their rocking chairs.

Where the lights were on, rooms often revealed a more intimate life: couples eating, women combing their hair, men reading their newspapers, and from every shanty-house floated the murmuring of radios.

Bessie and Erna Bolton's house was at a street corner. A single-storey affair. The light was on. The place was rather attractive, almost luxurious. Harold Mitchell and the musician were sitting on a sofa smoking cigarettes, while Erna, in a peignoir, was serving them ice cream.

Maggie Wallach was not there. Maybe she was working at the drive-in eatery, taking hot dogs and spaghetti out to the customers in their cars . . .

No mystery lurked anywhere. Everyone seemed to live in bright light. There were no worrisome shadows creeping around the houses, no curtains closed over snug interiors. Nothing but those cars going God knows where, without ever using their horns, stopping short at the crossroads as soon as the light turned red, later continuing on straight ahead.

He did not have dinner that night. When he went back downtown, the drugstores where he had counted on eating a sandwich were closed. Everything was closed, except for the three cinemas and the bars.

So, a little shamefaced, he went inside one of those bars, then another. He greeted the barman familiarly, as he'd seen others do, and perched on a stool.

Everywhere the same subdued music was playing. All

along the counter, shiny table-top jukeboxes swallowed up nickels. Turning a dial made the desired selection.

Could that be the explanation?

He was on his own and did what a man on his own can do.

When he returned to the hotel, he felt bitter and sluggish. He headed for the lift, then turned back to replace Cole's car key in the cubbyhole. His colleague might need his vehicle early the next morning.

'Good night, sir!'

'Good night!'

There was a Bible on the night table. In hundreds of thousands of hotel rooms, an identical Bible with a black cover sat waiting for the traveller.

In short: the bar or the Bible!

Class was being held upstairs again, and before Ezekiel's summons people were strolling out in the colonnade, already hot in the morning sun.

Everyone was wearing a clean shirt, and a refreshing shower had dispelled the drowsiness of the night.

And so, every morning, they began life anew, with a smile.

It was a little surprising, upon entering the courtroom, to see the five servicemen now out of uniform and wearing ample outfits of coarse blue cloth resembling pyjamas, which left their necks completely bare.

The result was that they didn't look so nice and clean-cut any more. Their irregular features were more noticeable, the slight asymmetries inspiring a feeling of uneasiness.

The blackboard had been set up and still showed the little puppet between the two chalk lines representing the railway tracks. This blackboard would again figure in the proceedings.

'Elias Hansen, of the Southern Pacific Railroad.'

He was not one of the train men Mitchell had asked to have testify. In a strong, even voice, this witness calmly explained what his job was. On behalf of the company, he investigated any thefts on the trains, accidents or violent deaths.

He was certainly of Scandinavian background. It was obvious from his demeanour. He was used to coroner's inquests and turned without any prompting towards the jury with the air of a schoolteacher explaining a difficult problem.

'I live in Nogales. I received a phone call shortly before six a.m. about the incident. I arrived at the site by car at six twenty-eight.'

'Did you see other cars near the scene of the accident?'

'The ambulance was still there, as well as four or five cars, some belonging to the police, the others to onlookers. A deputy sheriff was keeping people away from the railway tracks.'

'Was the train still there?'

'No. I met Deputy Sheriff Atwater, who had arrived earlier.'

He pointed to someone among the spectators, a man Maigret had already noticed without taking him for a colleague.

'What did you do?'

The man rose and stepped confidently to the blackboard, where he picked up a piece of chalk.

'May I erase this?'

Then he sketched in the highway and railway tracks, indicating the four cardinal points and the directions of Nogales and Tucson.

'First of all, at this spot here, Atwater pointed out some tyre tracks showing that a car had braked rather violently before parking by the roadside. As you know, the shoulder is sandy. Clearly visible footprints led away from the car, and we followed them.'

'The footsteps of how many people?'

'A man and a woman.'

'Can you indicate on the blackboard the approximate path they took?'

He did this in dotted lines.

'The man and woman appeared to walk side by side, without going in a straight line. They made several detours before reaching the tracks and stopped at least twice. Then they crossed the railway tracks at the spot I've marked with an X. On the other side, at a certain point, the trail disappears because the ground is hard and littered with pebbles. We picked it up again near the place where the woman was struck by the train. On the railbed, properly speaking, made of gravel, there were no footprints, but we found the woman's again a few yards away.'

'Not those of the man?'

'The man's as well, but they were not completely parallel. Someone had urinated at that spot, it was quite visible in the sand.'

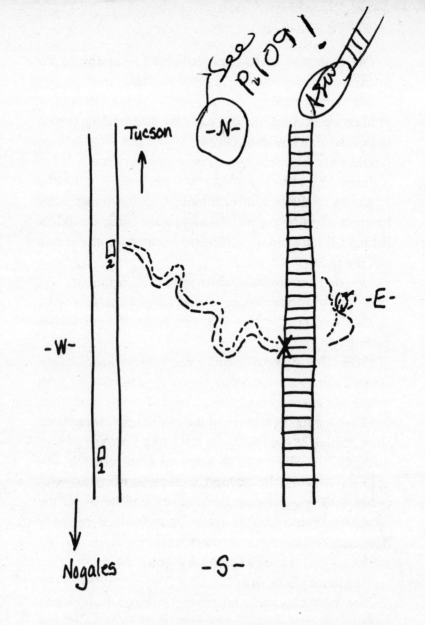

'Did you note if the footprints were ever superimposed at times?'

'Yes, sir. Here, and again here, twice, one of the man's prints covers one of the woman's, as if he had happened to swerve in behind her.'

'Did you find traces of the man going back towards the highway?'

'Not in a precise and continuous way. From this point on, the tracks become numerous and confusing, doubtless because of the train men, then the ambulance attendants and the police.'

'Do you have the string the engineer mentioned?'

He pulled it nonchalantly from his pocket. It was an ordinary piece of string that he obviously considered unimportant.

'Here it is. I found another piece fifty yards farther along.'

'Any questions, counsellor?'

'How many people were at the site when you arrived?'

'Perhaps a dozen.'

'Had other people already begun the investigation?'

'Deputy Sheriff Atwater and also, I believe, Mr O'Rourke.'

'You didn't find anything?'

'I came across a white leather handbag four or five yards from the tracks.'

'On the side with the footprints?'

'On the opposite side. It was partly embedded in the soft soil, as if it had been violently thrown at the moment of impact. We've seen that before. It's the result of centrifugal force.'

'Did you open the handbag?'

'I passed it on to Sheriff O'Rourke.'

'Was that the end of your investigation?'

'No, sir. I examined the highway for about half a mile in the directions of both Tucson and Nogales. Around one hundred and fifty yards along towards Nogales, I found distinct tyre tracks indicating that a car had pulled over on the right shoulder. There were many footprints, and the tyre tracks on the highway showed that the car had turned around there.'

'Are these tracks identical to the ones of the first car you spoke of?'

'No, sir.'

'How can you be sure?'

Hansen pulled a piece of paper from his pocket and read down a list of identifying marks from the tyres on the car that had made a U-turn. The four tyres were worn and were in fact of varying makes.

'Do you know to which car they belong?'

'I looked into that afterwards. They're the tyres on Ward's Chevrolet.'

'And the ones on the car where the footprints of the man and woman begin?'

'I don't think the sheriff will have any trouble finding that car. Tyres of that make are sold only on credit, with monthly payments.'

'Have you examined the taxi that drove to that spot with Sergeant O'Neil and Corporals Van Fleet and Wo Lee?'

'Yes, sir. That is not the other car. The taxi is equipped with Goodrich tyres.'

'Any questions, members of the jury?'

Recess. Maigret was already lighting his pipe, and Ezekiel, lighting his own, gave him a conspiratorial wink. After the deputy with the big revolver and the cartridge-studded belt led the five men in prison garb away to the arcade, they went one by one to the men's lavatory, where Maigret happened to find Ward and Mitchell.

Was he mistaken? He had the impression that when he'd pushed open the door, Sergeant Ward and Bessie's brother had suddenly stopped talking.

5. The Driver's Deposition

During that same recess, Maigret found himself alone with Mitchell in a corner of the ground-floor arcade, not far from the big, boxy red Coca-Cola machine.

Maigret felt as gauche and uncomfortable as a country boy accosting a pretty woman in a Paris street. At first he kept looking aside, clearing his throat. He tried to appear as casual as possible.

'Would you happen to have a photograph of your sister with you?'

What happened in the next few seconds was something Maigret had seen countless times before. Mitchell, who did not look particularly amiable to begin with, instantly took on the look of all thugs, from the tough guys of Paris to the gangsters of the American cinema. It was an animal reflex, a defence such people have kept, and it surfaces when wild beasts suddenly freeze, on the alert, tense, their fur bristling.

He stared hard at the big Frenchman, who did his best to remain relaxed.

A touch cravenly, hoping to appease the man, Maigret added: 'There are lots of questions that *they* don't seem eager to ask you.'

Mitchell was still wary, trying to see where he stood.

'It's as if they want it to be an accident.'

'That is what they want.'

'I'm in the same line of work. I'm in the French police. This case interests me for personal reasons. I'd have liked to see a photo of your sister.'

Tough guys are the same everywhere. Except that here they were less scornful, more embittered.

'Oh, so you don't believe, like those sons-of-bitches, that she went on purpose to lie down on the tracks and get run over by the train?'

He radiated fury and resentment. In the end he set down his bottle of Coca-Cola and pulled a big, worn wallet from his pocket.

'Look, here she is three years ago.'

It was a poor photo, taken at a country fair, in front of a painted backdrop. The three people looked pallid. They certainly weren't in the Southwest, because they were wearing thick winter clothing, and Bessie had a cheap fur collar on her coat, with a funny little round cap on her head.

She appeared to be fifteen, but Maigret knew she was younger. Her drawn, sickly little face was not without charm. She looked as if she were playing at being a woman, one proud to be going out with two men.

They must have been off on a spree that evening. The world was their oyster. Mitchell, barely an adolescent, hat down over his eyes, cigarette dangling from his lip, wore a look of defiance.

Her second companion was a bit older, eighteen or nineteen, rather big, rather fleshy.

'Who's that?'

'Steve. He married her a few weeks later.'

'What did he do?'

'At that time, he worked in a garage.'

'Where was that?'

'In Kansas.'

'Why did he get divorced?'

'To begin with he took off without warning, no one knew why. Those first few months, he sent her a little money; the money orders came from St Louis, and then from Los Angeles. Finally, one day he wrote her that it would be better if they divorced and he sent her the necessary papers.'

'Did he give a reason?'

'I think he didn't want to get my sister mixed up in anything. Six months later he was nabbed in a stolen-car ring. He's in San Quentin now.'

'Have you been to prison, too?'

'Just reform school.'

In France, it was easier. Maigret was used to such fellows and quickly made short work of the barrier between them.

Here, on unfamiliar ground, he advanced with caution, anxious not to spook his companion.

'Are you from Kansas?'

'Yes.'

'Your family was poor?'

'Yes, we were starving. Five of us, brothers and sisters barely a year apart. My father got himself killed in a truck when I was five.'

'He was a truck driver? Didn't the insurance pay up?'

'He worked on his own. He had an old truck and bought

vegetables out in the countryside to sell in the city. He was on the road every night. The truck wasn't completely paid for, and he had no insurance, of course.'

'What did your mother do?'

He fell silent.

'Whatever she could,' he muttered, shrugging. 'At six, I was selling papers and shining shoes in the streets.'

'Do you think Sergeant Ward killed your sister?'

'Definitely not.'

'He loved her?'

Another shrug, hardly noticeable.

'It wasn't Ward. He's not brave enough.'

'Did he really intend to get a divorce?'

'In any case, he wouldn't have killed her.'

'Mullins?'

'Mullins and Ward were never really apart long enough for that.'

He had taken back his photo and replaced it in his wallet.

Looking Maigret in the eye, he asked, 'If you ever did find out who killed my sister, what would you do?'

'I'd tell the FBI.'

'They have nothing to do with this.'

'I'd talk to the sheriff, to the attorney.'

'You'd do better to tell me about it.'

And still with that distant, slightly contemptuous air, he walked away, because Ezekiel could be heard upstairs, summoning the jurors.

Another confab between the coroner and the attorney, who then announced:

'I should like to depose the taxi-driver right away. He has been waiting since this morning and is losing his workday.'

It was almost always a surprise to see the witnesses emerge from the ranks of the public, for quite often they did not match the image you had of them. The taxi-driver, for example, was a short, thin man with an intellectual's big glasses, wearing light trousers and a white shirt like everyone else.

It was quickly established that he had been a taxi-driver for only one year, having previously been a professor of botany at a college in the Midwest.

'On the night of July 27 to July 28, you were hailed in front of the bus station by three airmen.'

'I learned that only from the newspapers, because they weren't in uniform.'

'Can you recognize them and point them out?'

The witness pointed immediately to O'Neil, Van Fleet and Wo Lee.

'Did you notice how they were dressed?'

'This one and that one were wearing blue jeans and white shirts, or at least light-coloured ones. The Chinese fellow had a violet shirt. I didn't notice the colour of his trousers.'

'Were they very drunk?'

'Not more than anyone else who gets picked up at three in the morning.'

'Do you know exactly what time it was?'

'We're supposed to write down every trip and note the time. It was three twenty-two.'

'Where did they tell you to go?'

'They asked me to drive towards Nogales and said they'd stop me along the way.'

'How long did it take you to get to the place where you did stop?'

'Nineteen minutes.'

'Did you hear their conversation while they were in the taxi?'

'Yes.'

'Who was talking?'

'Those two.'

He pointed to Van Fleet and Sergeant O'Neil.

'What were they saying?'

'That there wasn't any reason for their friend to stay with them, and he'd be better off keeping the taxi to get back to the base.'

'Did they say why?'

'No.'

'Who asked you to stop?'

'It was O'Neil.'

'Did they get out right away? There was no discussion about you waiting for them?'

'No. They did continue talking for a moment. They were trying to get their friend to return to Tucson with me.'

'Was it light out?'

'Not yet.'

'What did their friend say?'

'Nothing. He got out of the car.'

'Who paid for the ride?'

'The both of them. O'Neil didn't have enough money, and the other man chipped in the rest.'

'Didn't it seem strange to you that they had themselves driven out to the open desert?'

'A little.'

'You didn't encounter any cars along the way, either going or coming?'

'No.'

'Any questions, counsellor?'

'Thank you. I would like to ask Corporal Wo Lee a question.'

The airman returned to the witness stand, and the microphone was adjusted once more.

'Did you hear what the taxi-driver just said? Do you know why your friends insisted that you return to the base?'

'No.'

'What was your reason, yesterday, for not mentioning this?'

'I didn't remember it.'

He, too, was lying. He was the only one who hadn't been drinking, the only one whose statements had seemed reliable. Yet he had knowingly concealed their efforts to get rid of him.

'Are there other details that you left out of your testimony before the jury yesterday?'

'I don't believe so.'

'Yesterday, you stated that when you were walking along in the hope of finding Bessie, you were all separated. You were maintaining a certain distance one from another, along parallel lines. What was your position?'

'I walked along the highway.'

'You saw no cars go by?'

'I did not, sir.'

'Who was closest to you?'

'Corporal Van Fleet.'

'So Sergeant O'Neil was walking more or less along the tracks?'

'I think he was on the other side of them.'

'Thank you!'

The next witness was a highway patrol officer, tall and strong, impressive in his uniform.

The attorney had had him summoned, and he now questioned him.

'Tell us what you were doing on July 28 between three and four in the morning.'

'I went on duty at three o'clock, in Nogales, and drove slowly towards Tucson. Before reaching the village of Tumacacori, I passed a truck with the licence plate X-3233, belonging to a company in Nogales, returning empty from California. I parked for a few minutes in a side road so I could keep an eye on the highway, as per regulations.'

'Where were you at four in the morning?'

'I was approaching Tucson Airport.'

'Had you encountered any other vehicles?'

'No. Whenever we do see other vehicles, at night, we usually make a mental note of the licence plate numbers. In fact, we're supposed to check them against those on a list of stolen vehicles sent out to us. We automatically do that in our heads.'

'Did you see people walking along the edge of the highway?'

'No. If I had seen someone at that hour, I'd have slowed down and called out to them to see if they needed anything.'

'Did you see or hear a train on the tracks?'

'No, sir.'

'Thank you.'

So, in spite of Ward's claims, his Chevrolet had not been parked alongside the highway at that hour, with the two men asleep inside.

'Corporal Van Fleet, if you please?'

The attorney perked up, seeming suddenly to take charge of the proceedings, while O'Rourke kept leaning over him, talking softly.

Perhaps Maigret had been mistaken and they meant to press the inquiry all the way to the end, but according to some particular protocol?

'You maintain that when your friend's car stopped the first time, Sergeant Ward and Bessie walked away from the car together?'

'Yes, sir.'

Pinky was even more uneasy than he had been the day before. He did seem, however, to be trying to keep his oath to tell the truth and after each question, he still thought things over for a while.

'What happened next?'

'The car made a U-turn, and Bessie announced that she wanted to talk to Ward in private.'

'So you all stopped once more. Look at the blackboard. Does that cross mark the place, more or less, where the car pulled over a second time?'

'More or less. I think.'

'You did not leave the car, and neither did your friends, except for Ward and Bessie?'

'That's right.'

'And Ward returned alone. After about how long?'

'About ten minutes.'

'That's when he said, "Let her go to hell. That'll teach her."'

'Yes, sir.'

'Why did you and O'Neil try later on to get rid of Wo Lee?'

'We didn't try to get rid of him.'

'You did not discuss sending him back to Tucson in the taxi?'

'He hadn't been drinking.'

'I don't understand. Try to explain what you're thinking. It's because he hadn't drunk anything that you two wanted him to return to the base?'

'He doesn't drink, doesn't smoke. He's young.'

'Go on!'

'There's no reason for him to get into trouble.'

'What do you mean by that? So you were expecting, as of that moment, that you would get into trouble?'

'I don't know.'

'When you were walking along looking for Bessie, did you call her name?'

'I don't think so.'

'Is that because you thought she was not in any condition to hear you?'

This time the Dutchman, red-faced and perfectly still, did not answer. He stared straight ahead.

'Were you able at all times to keep your friend O'Neil within sight?'

'He was over by the tracks.'

'I am asking you if you kept him in sight the entire time.'

'Not the entire time.'

'Did you lose sight of him for long periods?'

'Rather long periods. It depended on the terrain.'

'Could you have heard him?'

'If he had shouted, yes.'

'But you could not hear his footsteps? You could not tell if he was stopping or not? Did you at any time go closer to the tracks?'

'I think so. We weren't necessarily walking in a straight line. We had to go around bushes, cacti.'

'Did Corporal Wo Lee move closer to the tracks as well?'

'I didn't see him.'

'Which one of you decided to turn around, when you were all three walking in the direction of Nogales?'

'O'Neil said that Bessie certainly couldn't have gone any farther. We told Wo Lee to walk alongside the highway.'

'And did you and O'Neil separate?'

'Yes, a little farther along in the desert.'

'While you were still with O'Neil, after having separated from Wo Lee, did you talk about Bessie?'

'No, we didn't talk about anything.'

'Were you still drunk?'

'Probably not as much.'

'Could you indicate on the blackboard the place where you went to hitchhike back to Tucson?'

'I don't know where, exactly. It was over there . . .'

'Thank you. Sergeant O'Neil, please.'

Two or three times, Maigret had sensed someone watching him. It was Mitchell, studying him to see how he was reacting.

'Do you have anything to change in your testimony from yesterday?'

'No, sir.'

Had this man, too, been born into poverty? He did not give that impression. He looked the type to have spent his childhood on some Midwestern farm, with hardworking and puritanical parents. In school, he must have been the star pupil.

'Why did you try to get rid of Wo Lee?'

'I did not try to get rid of him. I thought he was tired and ought to get back to the base. He doesn't have a strong constitution.'

'Did you ask him to walk beside the highway?'

'I don't remember.'

'When you were walking beside the tracks, looking for Bessie, did you ever call her name?'

'I don't remember.'

'Did you stop to urinate?'

'I think I did.'

'On the tracks?'

'I don't know, exactly.'

'Thank you. Coroner, we might do well to hear from Erna Bolton and Maggie Wallach and release them, as they've been expecting to testify since yesterday morning.'

Mitchell's companion was neither pretty nor ugly, a little low-slung, with coarse features. For her courtroom appearance she wore a dark silk dress, stockings, some costume jewellery. She had obviously tried her best to make a good impression.

When asked about her profession, she replied in a very low voice, 'I'm not working at the moment.'

And she tried not to look at O'Rourke, who seemed to know her well. No doubt she had had occasion to come up against him in the past?

'Did you share your apartment with Bessie Mitchell?'

'Yes, sir.'

'Sergeant Ward went there to see her several times. Were you present?'

'Not every time.'

'Did you ever see them quarrelling?'

'Yes, sir.'

'What were they fighting about?'

Now that the attorney had joined the fray, the coroner was playing with his adjustable armchair or staring at the ceiling while sucking on his pencil. It was quite hot, in spite of the air conditioning. Ezekiel had got up to go and close the venetian blinds, which cut the sunlight into thin slices. Sitting in front of the black woman with her baby and their large tribe, Maigret could smell her heady perfume.

Mitchell stared at his companion on the witness stand with the concentration of an eagle.

'Ward was angry at Bessie for flirting.'

'With whom?'

'With everybody.'

'With Sergeant Mullins, for example?'

'I don't know. He never came to the house. I saw him for the first time on July 27 at the Penguin Bar.'

'Wasn't there a fight, on July 24 or July 25, a dispute more violent than the others?'

'July 24. I was about to go out. I heard . . .'

'Tell us exactly what words you heard.'

'The sergeant shouted, "One of these days, I'll kill you, and that'll be best for everybody!"'

'Was he drunk?'

'He'd been drinking, but I don't think he was drunk.'

'Didn't you speak privately to Bessie during the evening of July 27?'

'Yes, sir. At one point, I took her aside to tell her, "You ought to watch out for that one."'

'Whom did you mean?'

'Mullins. And I said, "Bill is furious . . . If you keep this up, they'll get into a fight . . ."'

'What did she reply?'

'She didn't reply. She kept it up.'

'Kept what up?'

'Talking to Mullins.'

Perhaps the word 'talking' did not quite cover it.

'Who suggested continuing the party at the musician's place?'

'He did, Tony, the musician. He said we could. I think it was Bessie who'd asked him about it.'

'Was she drunk?'

'Not very. The usual amount.'

'Any other questions?'

It was Maggie Wallach's turn. With her round baby face and popping eyes, she resembled a large stuffed doll. Her skin was very white, and she had an unhealthy look about her.

Was she the musician's mistress? That was not made clear, no more than it had been for Mitchell and Erna Bolton.

'Where did you first meet Bessie Mitchell?'

'We worked at the same drive-in place, on the corner of Fifth Avenue.'

'For how long?'

'About the last two months.'

She was from a big-city slum and, when a little thing, she must have dragged her bare bottom around the neighbourhood doorsteps amid a pack of noisy, pitiless brats.

'You were present when she met Sergeant Ward?'

'Yes, sir. It was a little past midnight; he came in a car and ordered some hot dogs.'

'Who was with him?'

'I think it was Sergeant Mullins. They talked a long time. Bessie came to ask me if I wanted to get together with them later, and I told her that I wasn't free.

'After the men had gone, she wanted to know what I thought of Ward and said that he was coming back on his own to get her.'

'Did he?'

'Yes. Just before closing. They left together.'

'During the night of July 27, at the musician's place, did you see Ward rush in to the kitchen and hit Bessie?'

'No, sir. He did not hit her. I was behind him when he entered the kitchen. Bessie was drinking, and he snatched the bottle from her hands, almost threw it on the floor, got a grip on himself and set it on the table.'

'Was he furious?'

'He wasn't happy. He didn't like her to drink.'

'But wasn't he the one who'd taken her to the Penguin?'

'Yes, sir.'

'Why?'

'Probably because that's all there was.'

'Did Sergeant Ward, at that time, start quarrelling with Mullins? I'm still talking about the events in the kitchen.'

'I understand. He didn't say anything to him. He gave him a hard look, but didn't say a thing to him.'

Next! They seemed eager to wind everything up that day and the coroner was calling fewer recesses.

Tony Lacour, the musician, was puny and unassuming. The shape of his face always made him look as if he'd been crying or were about to do so.

'What do you know about the night of July 27?'

'I spent the evening at the Penguin Bar with them.'

'Weren't you working?'

'I'm not, for the moment. I wound up my gig at the Puerto Rico Club ten days ago.'

Just when Maigret was wondering what instrument he played, the attorney, who must have been wondering himself, asked that question. It was the accordion. Maigret would have bet on it.

'When a fight broke out between Ward and Mitchell at the Penguin, did you follow them outside? Do you know what they were fighting about?'

'I know that money was involved.'

'Didn't Mitchell reproach Ward for having relations with his sister, given that he was a married man?'

'Not in front of me, sir. Later, in my apartment, after the incident with the bottle, Mitchell told him that Bessie was inclined to drink, that it was a bad thing, that she was only seventeen and that in bars she could pass for twenty-three, otherwise they wouldn't have served her.'

'Was it you who suggested to the group that they go to your place?'

'Bessie admitted to me that she didn't feel like going home, and right away the others began talking about buying some bottles.'

'Did you give any cigarettes to Sergeant Ward?'

'I don't believe so.'

'Did you see anyone slip a pack into his pocket?'

'No, sir.'

'Was anyone, to your knowledge, smoking marijuana?'

'No, sir.'

'What time was it when they left your place?'

'About two thirty.'

'What did Harold Mitchell and Erna Bolton do?'

'They stayed.'

'Until morning?'

'No. Maybe another hour, hour and a half . . .'

'Was there talk about Sergeant Ward and Bessie?'

'Only about Bessie. Harold explained that his sister had

fallen into the habit of drinking and that it was terrible for her because she had a bad lung. And he said that when she was real young, she'd been in a sanitarium.'

'Did Mitchell and Erna leave in a car?'

'No, sir. They don't have a car. They left on foot.'

'Wasn't it around four in the morning?'

'At least that. It was starting to get light.'

Recess! Maigret again found the brother's eyes fixed upon him – and there was something just the slightest bit touching in his gaze.

Harold Mitchell's initial reaction to him had been an icy distrust, and perhaps he had answered Maigret's questions less out of hope than from a kind of defiance tinged with contempt.

He had been watching him the entire session and now seemed to be thinking, 'Who knows? Maybe he isn't like the others. He's a foreigner. He's trying to understand.'

Harold's attitude was hardly friendly yet, of course, but there was no longer that same insurmountable barrier between them.

'You hadn't told me she was tubercular,' Maigret murmured as they walked one behind the other towards the exit.

Harold merely shrugged. Perhaps he was ill as well? No, because in that case he would never have made it into the service. Erna Bolton was waiting for him out in the arcade. She did not take his arm. They did not speak to each other. She simply followed him, humble and docile, and her sagging bottom swayed like the business end of a laying hen.

With a gleam in his eye, O'Rourke headed with the attorney to the latter's office, while the five men in prison garb waited for the deputy to conduct them back to their cell.

Maigret hadn't listened to the end of the coroner's instructions. Would the afternoon session be upstairs or down? Over by the Coca-Cola machine, the female juror was eating a sandwich and would doubtless sit knitting on a bench in the plaza while waiting for the inquest to resume.

'Downstairs,' she replied when he asked her.

Harry Cole was waiting for him at the wheel of his car. There was someone sitting in the back seat, wearing the inevitable white shirt. He was smoking a cigarette.

'Hello, Julius! Not finished yet? Sit next to me. We'll go and grab a bite to eat.'

Only after the car door was closed did he add, by way of introduction, 'Ernesto Esperanza! He'll have to eat lunch with us, because I haven't anyone available to drive him to Phoenix before this evening and I don't much like handing him over to the county sheriffs. You hungry, Ernesto?'

'You bet, boss!'

'Here's your chance, then. It's the last restaurant meal you're likely to have for the next ten or fifteen years.

'I finally nabbed him,' he said simply, this time to Maigret. 'And it wasn't easy. He tried to get me with a forty-two. Open the glove box, you'll find his toy.'

The revolver was there, a big automatic, smelling of gunpowder. Maigret instinctively checked the magazine, where two cartridges were missing.

'He almost had me. Isn't that right, Ernesto?'

'Right, boss.'

'If I hadn't ducked down in time and tripped him up, I'd have been a goner. For six months now, I've been trying to catch him, and he's been doing his level best to get rid of me. How's it going, Ernesto? Your ribs still hurting you?'

'Not too much . . .'

To the others having lunch at the cafeteria, where they ate mutton chops and apple pie, they were simply three ordinary customers. Only on the next day did the Mexican's photograph appear in the newspapers under a big headline announcing that a major drug trafficker was under lock and key.

'What's happening with your five little Air Force fellows?' asked Cole, wiping his mouth with a paper napkin. 'Have you found the bad guy who put little Bessie on the tracks?'

Maigret didn't bother to frown. He was in a good mood that morning.

6. The Parade of Pals

Things were getting cosy. In the morning and especially after lunch, which some ate in the patio or the nearby plaza, people welcomed familiar faces, exchanged small gestures of greeting. Everyone knew where the seasoned spectators would sit, and even the five airmen did not seem to find the public's presence intrusive.

This intimacy was even more apparent downstairs, where the jurors sat on one of the public benches, next to curious onlookers, and where chairs were brought in when needed. The coroner would invariably look up at the big, noisy ceiling fan and frown. The water cooler and its paper cups were near Maigret, which meant that, sooner or later, everyone went by him.

Ever since he had casually patted the black woman's baby, she had saved his place for him and given him huge smiles.

As for Ezekiel, he always waited until the inquest had begun before springing his cigar or cigarette routine on a newcomer. He was a pretend bully with a childlike mischievous streak.

He would suddenly draw himself up, moustache quivering, arm outstretched, and cry, without any consideration for the ongoing interrogation, 'Hey, you!'

The entire courtroom would erupt in laughter. People turned around to see who had been caught.

'Put out your cigarette!'

Then, satisfied, he'd wink at his audience. He had enjoyed even greater success after spotting the attorney himself, who, returning after a recess, had forgotten he was still smoking.

'Hey, counsellor!'

Maigret could not believe that they would be winding up the inquest that very day, that in a few hours the five men and one woman of the jury would be ready to decide whether, yes or no, Bessie's death had been an accident.

If they decided yes, then the investigation would in effect be closed once and for all. If, on the contrary, they decided that her death was due to the criminal actions of one or more persons, Mike O'Rourke and his men would have plenty of time to work before the matter went to actual trial.

It was amusing: during lunch, Maigret had made a small discovery that made him smile and really pleased him, because in a way it let him get back a little at Harry Cole. The FBI man had behaved a little strangely, preening like a peacock, as if there had been a pretty woman with them, and Maigret had swiftly understood that the reason was Ernesto, the drug trafficker. Deep down, Cole felt instinctive consideration, almost admiration, for him, of the kind everyone in the States showed for anyone who succeeds, whether as a millionaire, a cinema star or a famous murderer. The Mexican had smuggled in $20,000 worth of drugs in a single haul, not to mention all his previous drug runs. Across the border, in mountains accessible only by plane, he had his own marijuana plantations.

Basically, the reason why the five Air Force men did not excite more interest was that, even if one of them did kill Bessie, he was not a criminal on a grand scale.

If he had held off the police, wielded a submachine gun, forced the mobilization of every officer and the use of tear gas to effect his capture, or if he had held up ten banks, or massacred several important ranchers' families, would there not have been a crowd outside the courtroom and on out to the middle of the street?

Did that not explain a lot of things? The goal was to win at the game, no matter what that game was.

A hard man, Mitchell was bound to be respected in his own small circle, whereas Van Fleet, with his choirboy face and wavy hair, was nobody. And the proof? His nickname was not Red, or Curly, but Pinky!

It was a deputy sheriff who now took the stand, Phil Atwater, the man who had arrived first on the scene and whom the inspector for the Southern Pacific had met there when he arrived.

He was not wearing his badge on his shirt. He looked ordinary, middle-aged, with the glum look of people with bad digestions and who always have someone sick at home.

'I happened to be in the sheriff's office shortly before five a.m., when the call came through. I took one of the cars and seven minutes later arrived at the scene of the accident.'

Maigret winced at that last word, and what followed would prove that he was not mistaken. Atwater, despite being a policeman, was the type who disdain the hum-drum factuality of real life.

'The ambulance drove up at about the same time as I did. Only the train crewmen were at the edge of the highway, along with a car that had pulled over a few minutes earlier. I posted one of the men I'd brought with me there, to keep any eventual onlookers from approaching the tracks. Right away, I found marks left by a car that had parked in that spot. I circled them with chalk, and on the sandy shoulder, with small sticks stuck in the ground.'

The fellow was the very model of a conscientious public servant and seemed to defy the whole world to find any fault with him.

'Did you not deal with the body?'

'Of course! I got busy with that as well. I even collected several pieces of flesh and part of an arm with a complete hand.'

He spoke in a condescending tone, as if the matter were strictly routine. Then he fumbled in his pocket and pulled out a small folded paper.

'Here are a few hairs. We have not had time to analyse them, but a first impression suggests that they're Bessie's.'

'Where did you find them?'

'Approximately where the impact took place. The body was dragged or rolled about twenty-five yards.'

'Did you find any footprints?'

'Yes, sir. I stuck bits of wood there to protect them.'

'Tell us what sorts of prints you found.'

'Women's footprints. I compared them with one of Bessie's shoes, and they matched.'

'There were no men's footprints near hers?'

'No, sir. In any case, not between the highway and the railway tracks.'

'And yet, later, when you followed the company inspector, Mr Hansen, he claims to have seen a man's footprints.'

'Probably mine.'

The deputy did not like to be contradicted and did not seem particularly fond of the Southern Pacific inspector.

'Will you show us, on the blackboard, the approximate track of the footprints?'

He looked at the previous drawing and, grabbing the rag, erased it. Then he made a fresh sketch of the tracks and highway, making a cross where the body had been found and another where it had been hit by the train. But he mistakenly put 'north' where 'south' should have been, and his wobbly drawing did not agree with Hansen's. According to Atwater, Bessie hadn't made nearly as many little detours and had stopped only once to change direction.

What did the jury make of these contradictions? They listened, watched attentively, clearly eager to understand and carry out their duty conscientiously.

'That's all you found on this side, meaning to the north of where Bessie died? Did you also look for footprints to the south, in other words, in the direction of Nogales?'

Atwater looked silently at his map and, as north and south were reversed, took some time to understand the question.

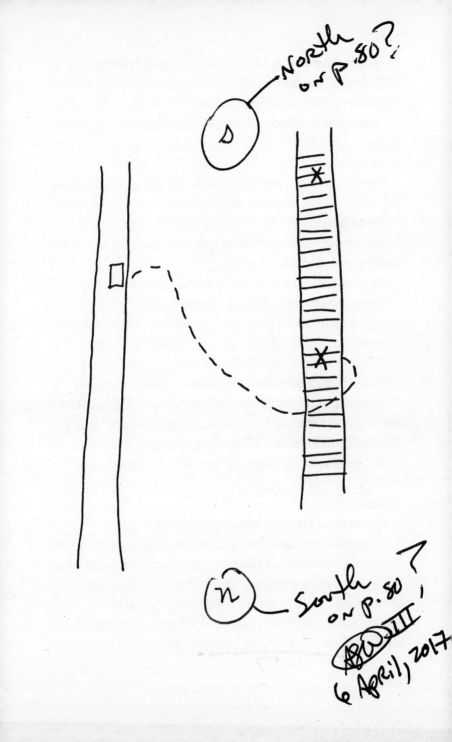

'No, sir,' he said at last. 'I did not think it necessary to look around towards Nogales.'

Free to go, he must have had work waiting at his office, because he left the courtroom immediately, very dignified and self-confident.

'Gerald Conley.'

He was another deputy sheriff, the one with so many cartridges in his belt and such a handsome revolver with a carved horn grip. He was chubby with a florid complexion, probably a popular fellow around Tucson and not a little proud of that.

'At what time did you arrive on the scene?'

'I was at home and wasn't contacted until ten past five. I arrived shortly after five thirty, without taking the time to have a cup of coffee.'

'Who was there already?'

'Phil Atwater was with the railway company inspector. Another deputy sheriff was maintaining order, because a few cars had stopped there. I saw the trail marked by pieces of wood and followed it from beginning to end.'

'In certain places, were the woman's footprints over the man's?'

'Yes, sir.'

'About how far from the highway was that?'

'Some fifteen yards away. The footprints in that spot clearly show that two people stopped there for some time, as if there had been some discussion.'

'After that, do the sets of footprints separate?'

'My impression is that the woman continued on alone. She was walking in zigzags. The man's footprints that turn up farther on are not the same as the first set.'

Maigret was starting to suffer again. Once more, he wanted to stand and speak up to ask specific questions.

That the five airmen should contradict themselves was only natural. They were like five schoolboys who had got themselves into a tight spot and who try, each on his own, to get out of it.

Besides, they had begun drinking at seven thirty that evening and were all drunk, except for Wo Lee.

But the police?

It seemed as if the deputies were settling personal scores, yet that didn't bother O'Rourke at all. Still sitting next to the attorney, still leaning over to make comments now and then, he was smiling beatifically.

'What did you do next?'

'I went south.'

Conley was clearly happy to land this direct hit at the colleague who had just left.

'Someone had urinated near the railway tracks.'

Maigret wanted to ask: 'A man or a woman?'

For after all, trivial though it may seem, a standing man and a squatting woman do not leave the same traces when they urinate, especially not in sandy soil.

The whole point turned on that, and no one seemed to have noticed.

No one had asked the doctor whether Bessie had made love that evening, either. No one had examined the underwear of the five airmen, or asked about anything beyond the colour of the shirts they were wearing . . .

Given the footprints leaving the car, Ward became the

prime suspect, on condition that these footprints were superimposed in at least one place. And on condition that, as in the testimony of the Southern Pacific inspector, these footprints continued on to the railway tracks. Atwater's deposition made Ward's guilt almost impossible – unless the crime had taken place during the second car trip.

With Conley, the deputy sheriff with the fancy revolver, everything changed yet again. Ward had supposedly followed Bessie for only about fifteen yards. But then, why did the sergeant claim he hadn't followed her at all?

'It's impossible,' continued Conley, 'to locate footprints on the railbed itself, which is stony, or on the soil immediately nearby, which is harder than the normal desert terrain. But walking towards the south and off to the right . . .'

'Towards the highway, in other words?'

'Yes, sir. Drifting right, I'm saying, I found other footprints.'

'Coming from which direction?'

'From the highway, more to the south.'

'Diagonally?'

'Almost perpendicularly.'

'A man's footprints?'

'Yes, sir. I put down markers. The length of the prints suggests to me that they belong to a man of medium height.'

'Where did that trail lead you?'

'To within around fifty yards of the place where the car stopped for the first time.'

Now there was no impediment to Ward's having told

the truth: that Bessie had gone off with Mullins and not come back.

The attorney must have been thinking the same thing.

'You didn't find any woman's footprints in that area?'

'No, sir.'

The hypothesis was already untenable.

'The trail vanishes once you get to the tracks?'

'Yes, sir. The person must have kept walking on the embankment, where footsteps leave no trace, as I said.'

Recess.

Twice O'Rourke went past Maigret out in the arcade, and both times he looked at him with a droll little smile. There must have been alcohol in the office he visited during each recess because afterwards it was on his breath.

Had Cole told him who the heavy-set, passionately attentive man in the audience was?

Was O'Rourke amused to see this colleague at a loss?

The juror with the wooden leg asked him for a light.

'Complicated, isn't it?' grumbled Maigret.

Had he used the wrong word? Had the fellow not understood? Or was he taking seriously the instructions not to discuss the case until a verdict was reached? In any case, the juror simply smiled and went off to stand before a lawn being watered by rotary sprinklers.

Maigret was sorry he had not taken any notes. The contradictions among the police officers' depositions did not interest him as much as those among the stories of the five airmen, who seemed more and more estranged from one another with each successive hearing.

'Hans Schmider!'

At times it was hard to tell why a witness was on the stand, and the game was to guess his profession. This man was portly; more precisely, his big belly swelled his shirt out like a flabby bag over his too-tight belt. His clinging trousers could not cover his navel, so he seemed to have short legs and an outsize torso.

His medium-length hair stuck out in every direction. His shirt was of dubious cleanliness. His arms and chest were hairy.

'You work in the sheriff's office.'

'Yes, sir.'

His strong voice and relaxed, almost familiar attitude suggested that he was used to such hearings.

'At what time were you apprised of the situation?'

'At around six that morning. I was asleep.'

'Did you leave immediately for the scene?'

'I swung by the office to pick up my gear.'

He was so at ease, leaning back in his chair, his belly prominently displayed, that he automatically pulled his cigarettes from his pocket, leaving Ezekiel just enough time to spring from his seat.

'Tell us what you saw.'

Schmider rose and with his hands in his pockets went to the blackboard to study the drawing there before erasing it. He had to bend down to pick the chalk up from the floor, thus pulling his trousers so taut that people thought they would split.

He marked the north, south, east, west; drew in the railway tracks, the highway, then a dotted line meandering extensively from the latter to the former.

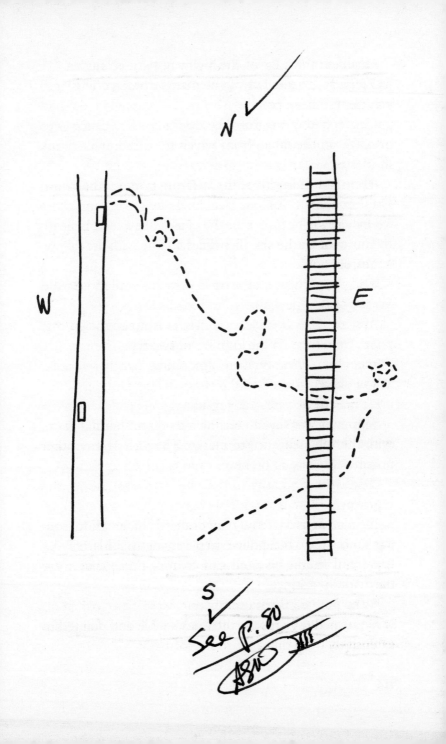

N

W

E

S

See P. 80

Finally, at the edge of the highway, two rectangles.

'Here, at point A, I saw tread marks from the car I'll call vehicle number one.'

He stepped down from the dais to fetch a rather large package on the table, from which he withdrew a chunk of plaster.

'Here is the imprint of the left front tyre, a rather worn Dunlop.'

On his own, he presented the object, like a cake, beneath the noses of the jurors, then did the same with the following three moulds.

'Did you compare these tread imprints with those from Ward's car?'

'Yes, sir. They are identical. There is no doubt on that point. Now, here are the imprints of two tyres from vehicle number two. These tyres are almost new, bought on credit. We've already visited all the stores selling Dunlops, but I don't believe we've had any results yet.'

Schmider was the lab technician on the sheriff's team, with the self-assurance to match. The idea of any other possible interpretation never even occurred to him.

'Did you find any more such marks along the highway?'

'When I arrived, I saw many other vehicles aside from the ambulance and police cars. I made moulds only of the tread marks pointed out to me, those that were particularly distinct.'

'Who pointed them out to you?'

He turned towards the attorney's table and pointed to O'Rourke.

'Did you make any other moulds?'

Schmider went back to his cardboard box as if it contained inexhaustible treasures, and everyone waited with both impatience and confidence, for everyone felt that from that box, the truth would emerge.

When he pulled out the impression of a shoe sole, the five airmen looked down in unison at their feet.

'This is a mould made about fifteen yards from the highway. It's from a man's shoe. The shoe is rather worn, with a rubber heel. Now here is the impression left by a woman's shoe I made right next to that other one. It matches exactly this shoe belonging to Bessie Mitchell, as you can verify.'

With the other hand, he waved a simple, ordinary, dark-reddish loafer, also much worn, with a flat heel. He walked both pieces of evidence past the jurors. With a little encouragement, he would have paraded them before the entire audience.

'Did you pursue further evidence regarding the man's shoe?'

'Yes, sir. I compared the imprint with the shoes of any sheriff or deputy who was at the scene.'

'Did you find a match?'

'No, sir. And Sergeant Ward, as I verified, was wearing high-heeled cowboy boots. Van Fleet, O'Neil and Wo Lee have smaller feet.'

Everyone waited. He knew it and savoured the delay.

'The size more or less matches Sergeant Mullins' feet, but the shoes he showed me do not have rubber heels.'

There was a sigh, as if in relief, in the line of airmen,

but Maigret could not tell which one of them had breathed it.

Schmider, who had carefully placed his moulds on the table, thrust his arm again into his box and pulled out, this time, a white leather handbag.

'This is the bag that was found a few steps from the railway tracks, partly buried in the sand.'

'Did anyone identify it?'

'No, sir.'

'Sergeant Mitchell!'

He stepped forwards. The bag was handed to him. He opened it and took out a kind of purse of red silk containing several coins.

'Is this your sister's handbag?'

'I'm not sure, but I recognize this purse Erna gave her.'

Sitting among the other spectators, Erna spoke up in agreement.

'It's her handbag. I was with her when she bought it, on sale, a month ago.'

A few people laughed. As the inquest had proceeded, people had grown so comfortable together that there was almost a circus atmosphere.

'Here are a handkerchief, two keys, a lipstick, a powder compact.'

'Aside from the coins, is there any folding money?'

'No, sir.'

And Erna spoke up again, without being asked:

'I remember that she'd forgotten her wallet.'

No papers. No identification of any kind. Maigret recalled a question he had already wondered about.

A woman's body, badly damaged, had been found on the railway tracks. Yet a few hours later, before the information was published in the newspapers, the sheriff's men had told Mitchell that his sister was dead.

Who had identified her? How?

Maigret looked glumly over at O'Rourke. This was the first time he had followed an investigation as a private individual, without knowing any behind-the-scenes information, and it frustrated him to feel that he was missing out on so much evidence.

Hadn't he done the same thing in Paris? How many times, to give himself free rein, to avoid some premature intervention, had he hidden – even from the examining magistrate – what he knew about a case?

Was O'Rourke at least going to press his advantages?

Did he really want to discover the truth and, above all, reveal it?

There were moments when Maigret doubted it – and others when he thought his colleague, who knew his job, would do what needed to be done in his own good time.

One last piece of evidence remained in the box, and Schmider brought it out at last. It was another mould, another plaster footprint.

'This cast was made to the south of where Bessie died.'

In other words, from the trail of prints only Gerald Conley had described.

'It's a size nine, meaning a medium size, verging on small. Corporal Wo Lee wears an eight. Sergeant O'Neil and Corporal Van Fleet wear a nine and a nine and a quarter, respectively. The shoes they showed me did not display the same signs of wear.'

Once more, Maigret almost rose for permission to speak, forgetting that he was not on home ground.

The clock above the door, which was open and crowded with curious onlookers, read four thirty. On both preceding days, the hearings had been adjourned at around five o'clock.

Twice already, documents had been brought for the coroner to sign, which he had done without interrupting the interrogations.

'Any questions, members of the jury?'

It was the black man who spoke up.

'Did the witness take any impressions of tread marks from the taxi?'

'None were pointed out to me.'

'Doesn't he know anything about the third car, the one that took the three airmen back to the base?'

'When I arrived on the scene, several vehicles were already there, and while I was working other cars arrived.'

The coroner looked at the clock.

'Jurors, the chief deputy sheriff is our only remaining witness before you begin deliberations. I'm wondering if we shouldn't keep going to wind this up today.'

O'Rourke raised his hand.

'May I be allowed a remark here? My deposition will not necessarily be a long one, but it is possible that, if we wait until tomorrow morning, a new witness will provide us with interesting information.'

Maigret could breathe again. He breathed so deeply,

with such an air of relief, that two of his neighbours looked around at him. He had been afraid that the jurors would be sent off to deliberate with such ragged and contradictory material.

Above all, it seemed incredible that this inquest would be closed without further discussion of the third car, to which the black juror had just alluded, the one that had taken the three airmen back and had apparently yet to be found.

Was it the one with the tyres bought on credit? Why, at least twice, had the attorney asked witnesses if the body of the car had been in good condition and whether they had noticed any signs of an accident?

The coroner turned questioningly to the jurors, who all, except for the woman, quickly nodded their assent.

Thus, for one more day, they would be something other than ordinary citizens. As if to compound their delight, a photographer crouched down in front of them – and a flash shot through the courtroom.

'Tomorrow, Courtroom Two, nine thirty.'

Maigret must have been in the photo, because he was only two people away from the foreman of the jury.

For about an hour, he had been anxious to get down to work with pencil and paper, which was unusual for him. He needed to take stock of the situation and felt that it would not take him long to eliminate most of the hypotheses.

'They didn't question the other men on the train,' said someone close to him.

It was Mitchell, in a bad mood.

'The engine driver, who was at the left in the locomotive, could see only the left side of the tracks, where my sister's legs were. His assistant, on the right, saw the upper part of the body. I've asked again that he be called to the stand.'

'What did they say?'

'That they'll do so if they see any need to.'

'How did they recognize your sister?'

This time, Mitchell looked at him in amazement, and with that simple question Maigret must have lost considerable prestige in his eyes, because he simply shrugged and went off into the crowd.

Maigret had understood. Wasn't it obvious that a girl like Bessie had already been involved with the police? Tucson must have had a few dozen more like her, basically, and the law probably kept an eye on them.

That suddenly reminded him of the men on those barstools, all evening long, staring dolefully at what were essentially girly calendars. And it reminded him of the cars he had noticed, parked in the shadows, in which couples were probably holding their breath as he passed by . . .

Harry Cole hadn't said when he would meet him, but Maigret was sure he would run into him any time now. It was the FBI man's way of impressing him, a way of saying: 'I let you come and go, but as you see, I always know where to find you.'

Just to be difficult, Maigret went into a bar instead of returning to the hotel, and the first words he heard were: 'Hello! Julius!'

Cole was there, and Mike O'Rourke was sitting next to him with a glass of beer.

'You know each other? Not yet? Detective Chief Inspector Maigret, a famous policeman in his country. Mike O'Rourke, the wiliest chief deputy sheriff in Arizona.'

Why did these people always seem to be making fun of him?

'How about a beer, Julius! Mike tells me you've been following the depositions assiduously and that you must have your own thoughts on the matter. I've invited him to have dinner with us. I suppose that's fine with you?'

'I'm delighted.'

That wasn't true. He would have appreciated the gesture the next day, when he would have had time to go over what he knew. Now, he felt even more awkward and stupid in that the others seemed in excellent humour, as if they had something sneaky in mind.

'I'm sure,' observed O'Rourke as he wiped his lips, 'that Inspector Maigret finds our investigative methods downright rudimentary and naive.'

For his counter-attack, Maigret inquired: 'Did the waitress at the Penguin Bar give you any helpful information?'

'She's a pretty girl, isn't she! Her background's Irish, like mine, and you know, the Irish always get along well together.'

'Was she at the Penguin on the evening of July 27?'

'That was her day off. She knew Bessie real well and knows Erna Bolton and a few of the fellows.'

'Including Mullins?'

'I don't think so. She hasn't mentioned him to me.'

'Wo Lee?'

'Not him, either.

That left Corporal Van Fleet and Sergeant O'Neil – who was an Irishman as well, like the chief deputy sheriff.

'Have you found the third car?'

'Not yet. I'm still hoping we'll find it before tomorrow morning.'

'There are some things I don't understand.'

'There would certainly be more things I wouldn't understand if I were following an investigation in Paris.'

'Back home, the real investigation does not take place in public.'

O'Rourke shot him an amused look.

'Or here, either.'

'I suspected as much. But each of your men still comes and says whatever he feels like saying.'

'Now that, that's another story. Don't forget that everyone gives evidence under oath, and that in the United States this oath is a very serious matter. Perhaps you've noticed, though, that they answer only the specific questions they get asked!'

'What I particularly noticed is that there are questions they do not get asked.'

Mike O'Rourke clapped him on the shoulder.

'OK! You've figured it out! After we've had dinner, you can ask me all the questions you want.'

'And you'll answer them?'

'Probably. As long as I'm not under oath . . .'

7. The Inspector's Questions

It was not Harry Cole, but O'Rourke who seemed to be their host. Instead of taking his guests to a restaurant, he had brought them to a private club downtown.

The premises were new, inviting, surprisingly modern. The bar was probably the best-stocked watering hole Maigret had ever seen: while they had their cocktail, he was able to count forty-two different whiskies, not to mention seven or eight labels of French cognac and some authentic Pernod, unseen in Paris since 1914.

Lined up facing the bar, with their familiar symbols of plums, cherries and apricots, were the perfectly polished slot machines. Just as Maigret was about to drop in his usual nickel he noticed that these machines took either silver dollars, half-dollars or quarters.

'I thought these machines were illegal,' he remarked. 'The day I arrived, in fact, I read in a Tucson paper that the sheriff had impounded a number of them.'

'In public places.'

'And here?'

'We're in a private club.'

O'Rourke had a merry look in his eyes. He seemed happy to enlighten his colleague from overseas.

'You see, there are many private clubs, at every level of society, so to speak. This one is neither the most elegant nor the most exclusive. Four or five rank higher, and a whole slew are lower.'

Looking around the vast dining room where they would be eating, Maigret began to understand why he had noticed a relative lack of restaurants.

'No matter what your job, you have your own club, and moving up in society you go from club to club.'

'Meaning that everyone can also play the slots.'

'Just about.'

And with a sidelong wink, O'Rourke dropped a big new silver dollar into a slot, then casually swept up the four identical coins that tumbled down.

'There's a dice game downstairs that's our equivalent of your roulette. We play poker, too. Don't you have clubs in France?'

'A few, only among certain social classes.'

'Here we even have a club for railway workers and post office employees.'

Maigret exclaimed in surprise.

'Then – will you please tell me what all your bars are for?'

Harry Cole was drinking his double whisky as if performing a ritual.

'First off, they provide neutral ground. A man doesn't always want to meet people in his *own* category.'

'Just a minute! Stop me if I'm mistaken. Don't you mean, rather, that a man doesn't always want to *behave* the way he's obliged to among people of his own category? I suppose that here, for example, it's pretty poor form to drink yourself under the table?'

'Correct. For that there's the Penguin Bar or its like.'

'I understand.'

'There are also those who don't belong to any category, in other words, to any club at all.'

'Those poor folks!'

'Not only people who don't have money, but those who don't conform to the customs of a specific social class. Listen to this! In Tucson, which is a major city, there's a club for folks of Mexican background who've been here for several generations. In that club, speaking Spanish is frowned on! Those who still speak it or speak English with an accent go to a different club, for newcomers. Have a drink, inspector!'

All around them, the setting and service were those of a deluxe restaurant in Paris. One of the sheriffs ate his meals there almost every day.

'Tell me, do the airmen at the base have their club as well?'

'They have several.'

'When they want to behave in a certain way, are they also obliged to go off to the bars?'

'Exactly.'

'Our friend Julius is catching on,' remarked Cole, eating hungrily.

'Many things are still a mystery to me.'

There was wine on the table, French wine that O'Rourke had had the delicacy to order without mentioning it. This big man of unsophisticated appearance was not without finesse. On the contrary, and as the evening went on, Maigret liked him more and more.

'Would it bother you if I talked about the inquest?'

'That's why I'm here.'

It had been a set-up. Perhaps it was O'Rourke who had asked Cole to introduce him to his colleague?

'If I understand correctly, your position here is the same one I hold in Paris. The sheriff, your superior, corresponds roughly to the head of the Police Judiciaire.'

'Except that the sheriff is elected.'

'As for the attorney, he's rather like our public prosecutor. And the deputy sheriffs you have under you are the equivalent of my brigade officers and inspectors.'

'I believe that's about right.'

'I've noticed you feeding the attorney most of his questions. You're doubtless also the one who's been preventing certain other questions from being put to the witnesses . . .'

'Correct.'

'Had you already questioned those witnesses?'

'Most of them.'

'And you asked them *all* the questions?'

'I did my best.'

'What's Corporal Van Fleet's family background?'

'Pinky? His parents run a large farm out in the Midwest.'

'Why did he join the Air Force?'

'His father insisted that he work the farm with him. Pinky did so, unwillingly, until two years ago, when, one fine day, he left and joined up.'

'O'Neil?'

'Both his parents are teachers and very respectable people. They wanted to make him into an intellectual and felt let down when he wasn't at the top of his class. And he'd had enough of it as well. Whereas Van Fleet went from the countryside to the city, O'Neil went from a small town out to the country. For almost a year, he worked picking cotton down south.'

'Mullins?'

'When quite young, he had some trouble with the police and was sent to reform school. His parents died when he was ten or twelve. The aunt who took care of him is a strict and unbearable creature.'

'Is the doctor's report complete?'

'I don't know what you mean.'

'Five men spent much of the night drinking with one woman. This woman was found dead on the railway tracks. Well, not for a moment has anyone at the inquest ever brought up what might have happened between the woman and one or more of those men.'

'That is never brought up.' — *Insanity!*

'Not even in your office?'

'In my office, it's different. I can tell you that the autopsy was as complete as could have been desired.'

'The result?'

'Yes!'

'Who?'

It was a little as if, until now, Maigret had seen only a kind of painted picture of the case, like the backdrop in a photography studio. That was what the public saw, and it seemed to satisfy them.

Now real people, and what they had really done, were slowly replacing the artificial image.

'It didn't happen out in the desert.'

'At the musician's place?'

That visit to the musician's apartment had been bothering Maigret all along.

'First, the doctor discovered that Bessie had had sex with a man during the night, but that this had happened rather a while before her death. You know that in such a case there is a procedure similar to a blood test that can sometimes tell if this or that man has had relations with someone. I spoke first to Ward, and he went scarlet. It wasn't fear, but jealousy and rage. He jumped up, shouting, "I knew it!"'

'Mullins?'

'Yes. He confessed right away.'

'In the kitchen?'

'It was planned in advance. He had confided to Erna Bolton that he was mad with desire for Bessie. For some reason or other, Erna doesn't much like Sergeant Ward. She promised Mullins, "Maybe later, at the musician's place . . ."'

'She admitted that she kept watch near the kitchen. She's the one who warned the couple that Ward was coming. And it was to fool him that Bessie thought fast enough to grab a whisky bottle and take a swig from it.'

Now Maigret saw more clearly why some witnesses were thinking hard before answering any questions, weighing every word.

'Don't you think these details would have interested the jurors?'

'It's the result that counts, isn't it?'

'And you'll get the same result?'

'I'm making sure of it.'

'Is it from a sense of decency that you avoid all questions of a sexual nature?'

As he was asking that question, Maigret remembered the slot machines in the bar and thought he understood.

'I suppose you want to avoid setting any bad examples?'

'That's about it. In France, if what I've heard is true, you do precisely the opposite. The newspapers tell all about the shenanigans of government ministers and VIPs. Then, when some ordinary little guy is unfortunate enough to do the same, you toss him in the slammer. Any more questions, inspector?'

'If I'd had time, I would have written them down. Does Erna claim that her friend Bessie was in love with Mullins?'

'No. She thinks, as I do, that Bessie was truly in love with Sergeant Ward.'

'But she wanted Mullins?'

'When she'd been drinking, she wanted any man.' Yuk!

'Did that happen to her often?'

'Several times a week. And on Ward's side, it was romance. When he didn't come to see her, he wrote her every day and sometimes talked on the telephone with her for half an hour.'

'Did she hope to marry him?'

'Yes.'

'And he?'

'That's difficult to say. I'm sure he answered me sincerely. He's a decent enough fellow, really. He got married the way lots of young folks get married around here, in a matter of days. You meet a girl. You think you're in love because you want her and you go looking for a marriage licence.'

'I noticed the court avoided summoning the wife.'

'Why bother? She's not in good health. She's having trouble raising her two children. She's expecting a third, and that's what was holding Ward back. He would really have liked to marry Bessie and at the same time he was afraid of hurting his wife.'

Maigret had not been mistaken in comparing these grown men to schoolboys. They played at being tough. They thought they were tough. A hoodlum from La Bastille or Place Pigalle would have scorned them as choirboys.

'Was it you, chief, who identified the body?'

'My men had done it before me. Bessie went through my office five or six times.'

'Because she was engaging in prostitution?'

'You always use words that are too specific, and that's why it's so hard to answer you. For example, when she worked at the drive-in restaurant, Bessie earned about thirty dollars a week. Well, the apartment she shared with Erna cost them only sixty dollars a month.'

'Did she earn anything on the side?'

'Not necessarily in cash. She got taken out to eat and drink. A cocktail costs fifty cents! A whisky, the same.'

'Are there lots like her in the city?'

'At different levels. There are some you take out for spaghetti at a drive-in and others whom you invite for a chicken dinner in a nice restaurant.'

'Erna Bolton?'

'Mitchell keeps a close eye on her. It would cost her a lot to cheat on him, and I'm convinced he'll marry her one of these days. They aren't little saints, but they're not bad people.'

'Did Sergeant Mitchell know that his sister and Mullins had had sex in the kitchen?'

'Erna took him aside to tell him about it!'

'How did he react?'

O'Rourke began to laugh.

'I wasn't there, inspector. I only know what he felt like telling me. Did you know that he was his sister's guardian and that he took this seriously?'

'By letting her sleep with any man she fancied?'

'What would you have had him do? He couldn't be with her night and day. She absolutely had to earn her living, and she wasn't well educated enough to work in an office. He tried to have her work as a salesgirl in a five-and-ten-cent store, but she didn't last longer than a day because she kept chatting with the customers and made mistakes in her arithmetic. Mitchell saw Ward as better than nothing, and he might have wound up marrying her. Mullins would have been an improvement, since he was single.'

Now it was Maigret's turn to laugh. The characters of all these people were changing right before his eyes with every revelation O'Rourke made.

Brandy had been served, a vintage bottle, which the chief deputy sheriff was proud to offer his guest. O'Rourke, who had heard that cognac must be decanted before it is drunk, held his glass reverently in the palm of his big hand.

'To your health!'

What surprised Maigret was not the leniency of men like his police colleague, or like Harry Cole, who brought his prisoner along for lunch in a good restaurant.

That kind of indulgence was common at Quai des Orfèvres, too. In Paris there were certain bad characters whom Maigret knew by heart, ran into now and then, and to whom he sometimes said: 'You've gone too far again, my friend, and I've got to arrest you. It'll do you good to meditate in the shade for a few months.'

What did astonish him was the attitude of the jurors, the public. For example, when the witnesses had described the drunken saga of that night and mentioned the number of rounds, no one had even blinked.

Those people seemed to understand that it takes all kinds to make a world and that a certain percentage of any society will always fall by the wayside.

At the top of the criminal heap, there are the major mobsters, who are almost indispensable since it's thanks to them that everyone can obtain what is forbidden by law.

Those gangsters need killers to settle their accounts among themselves.

Not everyone can belong to a club catering to a certain social class. Not everyone can climb the social ladder.

There are those who descend it. There are those who are born at the very bottom. There are the weak, the ones born unlucky, as well as those who become bad guys to brazen it out and believe in spite of everything that they're still good for something.

And it was all this that these ordinary people seemed to understand.

'Does Van Fleet have a mistress?'

'Are you asking me if he sleeps more or less regularly with a woman?'

'If you prefer.'

'No. It's more difficult than you think. Aside from a Bessie or an Erna Bolton, a woman, in that situation, always manages to get herself married. Bessie had almost made it. Erna will.'

'So that he could count only on the odd opportunity?'

'Rare opportunities, yes.'

'And O'Neil?'

'O'Neil as well! Let me point out, by the way, that Ted O'Neil, all appearances to the contrary, is the most timid of all. He feels out of place. He isn't comfortable in his own skin! He had a strict upbringing. I wonder if he doesn't sometime miss the paternal homestead and that whole righteous world that has now shut him out.'

'His parents don't write to him?'

'They no longer wish to know him.'

'Wo Lee?'

'When you have lived in a city along with a few hundred Chinese, you'll find that you're better off not trying to understand them. I think Wo Lee is a good little boy, and he wants to succeed. He's proud of his uniform. He'll get himself bravely killed in the next war.'

Harry Cole, who had hardly said a word, watched them both with an enigmatic smile.

But now he spoke up: 'I know a little about the Chinese.'

'What do you think of them?'

'Nothing!' he said, tongue in cheek.

Most of the diners had finished eating; from the now crowded bar came loud chatter and the clinking of glasses. People were playing cards in a neighbouring room.

'Question?'

'Yes. I'm not sure how to ask it. I keep coming back to the fact that they were five men and one woman and they had been drinking. Mullins, you told me, had given in to temptation. He got want he wanted. That left Ward's three other pals. Don't you think a big red-faced boy like Van Fleet, a solid young man like O'Neil wanted her as well?'

'Quite possibly.'

'Don't you think she played the same game with them as she did with Mullins?'

'Probably. She must have got them going, if that's what you mean.'

'Do the Chinese, like blacks, have a certain predilection for white women?'

'Your turn, Harry.'

'I don't think it's a real preference. Their natural inclination would be for their own women. But with them it's a question of pride.'

'So,' continued Maigret, returning to his theme, 'they were five men and one woman in a car. All squeezed together in the back seat, as I remember, in the dark, there were O'Neil, Bessie and Wo Lee. Wait! I've started at the wrong end. You said Ward was jealous. He knew Bessie's temperament and her behaviour when drunk. Yet he's the one who organized this night out with his pals.'

'You don't understand?'

'I think I do, but I'd like to know if my rationale seems logical to Americans.'

'Ward was rather proud of himself: he, a married man, had what you'd call a mistress. Can you imagine what prestige that gave him with regard to his friends?'

'He was willing to run the risk?'

'He wasn't thinking of the risk, only of impressing them. You'll remember that at a certain point he became worried and tried to keep Bessie from drinking.'

'He didn't seem to be jealous of anyone but Mullins.'

'He wasn't that far wrong. He saw Mullins as the handsome guy who attracts women. He wasn't so worried about the other two, who were a head shorter than he is, still less about Wo Lee, who's only a child.'

'You admit that it's some sort of exhibitionism?'

'I've heard that in Paris and elsewhere, at the opera or like places, the snootiest people proudly show off their wives or mistresses in very low-cut dresses.'

'Do you think something happened in the car that made Bessie decide not to go on to Nogales?'

'One explanation springs to mind, but I don't know if it's the right one. After bursting in to the kitchen, Ward became nervous and ill-tempered. He made Bessie change places and sit in the back of the car to get her away from Mullins. By the same token, he was moving her away from himself. It was a kind of sulk. She might well have sulked right back at him.'

'What if something scared her?'

'Some move made by O'Neil or Wo Lee, in a car carrying six people? Don't forget, inspector, that everyone except Wo Lee was pretty drunk.'

'Is that why their testimonies don't match?'

'And also because, I admit, they each feel more or less under suspicion. Besides, friendship is involved. O'Neil and Van Fleet are almost inseparable, and you've noticed that their depositions are almost identical. Wo Lee tries to deal tactfully with everyone, because he can't bear to be a tattletale.'

'Why did Ward claim that Bessie didn't get back in the car after the first stop?'

'Because he's afraid. Don't forget, this business puts him in trouble up to his neck. He's got a wife and children. His wife will probably file for divorce.'

'He stated that Bessie went off with Sergeant Mullins.'

'What proves she didn't?'

'Your deputies contradict one another as well.'

'Each of them is under oath and says what he believes to be the truth.'

'The Southern Pacific inspector seems to know his job.'

'He's a good man.'

'Conley?'

'A fine fellow.'

'Atwater?'

'A complete jackass.'

He did not mince words in rating his subordinates.

'And Schmider?'

'A first-rate technician.'

'You really hope to find the car that took the three men back to the base?'

'I'd be surprised if it isn't parked in front of my office tomorrow morning, because this afternoon we obtained the address of the garage that sold the set of tyres.'

'That's why the inquest was adjourned until tomorrow?'

'That, and because the jurors will be more alert.'

'You think they've understood some of it?'

'They've been paying close attention. At this point, they're probably a little lost. Tomorrow, it should be enough to present them with more evidence, if we have any.'

'And if you don't?'

'They'll decide according to their consciences.'

'Doesn't this system allow many guilty people to go free?'

'That's better than locking up the innocent, don't you think?'

'Why did you go back to the Penguin Bar yesterday?'

'I'll tell you. Bessie, who lived close by, went there almost every night. I wanted to make a list of all the men she was meeting there.'

'Did the waitress give you some interesting information?'

'She told me that Van Fleet and O'Neil had come by several times.'

'With Ward?'

'No.'

'Did they ever go out with Bessie?'

'No. Bessie didn't like them.'

'Does that mean Bessie couldn't have made a date with

them? O'Neil could have talked to her in the car and asked her to get rid of the others.'

'I thought about that.'

'She announces that she does not want to continue on to Nogales, picks a fight with Ward, refuses to get back in the car and waits for the other two in the desert. They leave their other friends when they get to Tucson, never suspecting that Ward and Mullins mean to go back to where they had been. They try to get rid of Wo Lee, who isn't in on the plan, then take a taxi.'

'And they kill her?'

'I believe I would have had the two men's underwear examined.'

'That was done. The results were negative for Van Fleet, if I get what you mean. It was too late for O'Neil, as his underwear had already gone off to the laundry by then.'

'Do you think Bessie was murdered?'

'The thing is, chief inspector, here we never believe someone is guilty until we have proof. Every man is presumed innocent.'

Maigret shot back, half seriously, half in jest: 'Every French person is presumed guilty. Nevertheless, I bet it was you who had those five locked up on a charge of inciting a minor to drink.'

'Did they get her to drink, yes or no? Did they admit it?'

'Yes, but . . .'

'So they broke the law, and that works out for me, because it simplifies my task to have them in jail. I don't have that many men at my disposal. I would have had to keep them all under surveillance. And I think you now know about as much as I do regarding all this. If you have any more questions, I'm still available.'

'Was it just after learning of his sister's death that Mitchell claimed she'd been murdered?'

'That was his first reaction. Don't forget that he knew she had had sex with Mullins in the kitchen and that Ward had almost caught them at it.'

'No!'

'What do you mean?'

'Mitchell has never suspected Ward. Anyway, it's not Ward he suspects at the moment.'

'He told you so?'

'That's what he gave me to understand.'

'Then you know more than I do, and perhaps I'd best have a talk with him. Be that as it may, I have to get to the office now. Are you staying with the inspector, Harry?'

Maigret wound up on the street with Cole, whose car, as usual, was not far off.

'Where do you feel like going, Julius?'

'To bed.'

'You don't think this might be the moment for a nightcap?'

That was the thing: they had just left a pleasant club where every kind of drink in the world had been on offer. Cole knew everyone there. They could have talked and imbibed their fill.

Yet, once outside, Cole wanted to go and prop up some anonymous bar.

Perhaps it had something to do with the attractive power of sin?

Maigret almost left his companion and returned to the hotel, because he really did want to go to bed. A kind of cowardice led him to stay with Cole, who pulled up a little later, naturally, across the street from the Penguin.

It was almost deserted, that evening. Music was coming from the jukebox, its lights gleaming in the habitually dim interior.

Two couples were sitting at a table near the jukebox: Harold Mitchell with Erna Bolton and the musician with Maggie.

Seeing Maigret enter with the FBI man, Mitchell raised an eyebrow and began talking quietly with his companions.

'Are you married?' Maigret asked Cole.

'And the father of three. They're off in New England, since I'm posted here for only a few months.'

There was a hint of homesickness in his eyes, and he downed his drink in one go.

'What do you think of the club?' he asked in turn.

'I did not expect it to be so luxurious.'

'There are better ones. At the Country Club, for example, they have golf, several tennis courts, a magnificent swimming pool.'

After signalling the barman for a refill, Cole continued.

'A person can eat much better and for less money than in the restaurants. Everything is of good quality. Except that, you have to admit . . . There's no word in English. I think that in French you'd say, it's *emmerdant*, right?'

Such strange people! They saddled themselves with strict rules. And they tried conscientiously to follow them for so many hours per day, or days per week, or weeks per year.

Did they all feel the need to escape from them at some point?

It was much later, near closing time, that Cole – who had drunk a great deal and who that day was aggressive only towards himself – confessed his secret.

'You see, Julius, for the world to go around, it's essential that people live in a certain way. You have a comfortable house, electric appliances, a luxurious car, a well-dressed woman who gives you beautiful children and keeps them clean. You belong to your parish and your club. You earn money and work each year to increase the amount. Isn't that the way it is all over the world?'

'Perhaps your country has perfected this system.'

'Because we're richer. Here we have poor people with their own cars. The blacks who pick cotton almost all have an old car. We have reduced the down-and-outers to a minimum. We are a great people, Julius.'

And when Maigret replied, 'I am convinced of that,' he was not simply being polite.

'Still, there are moments when the comfortable house, the smiling wife, the well-scrubbed children, the car, the club, the office and bank account are not enough. Does that happen back in your country, too?'

'I believe that happens to everybody.'

'Well, Julius, I'm going to give you my remedy, which a few million of us know and use. You walk into a bar like this one, which one doesn't matter, for they are all alike. The barman calls you by your first name or some other first name if he doesn't know you, it's not important. He pushes a glass towards you and fills it whenever he sees it empty.

'Sooner or later, someone you don't know will tap you on the shoulder and tell you the story of his life. Most of the time, he shows a snapshot of his wife and kids and finally confesses to you what a fucking pig he is.

'Sometimes a fellow who gets gloomy on the booze looks at you funny and, for no apparent reason, punches you in the face.

'It doesn't matter. At any rate, you'll be ushered outside at one in the morning because it's the law, and the law is still the law.

'You try to get home without knocking over any lamp-posts, because you risk going to prison if you drive drunk.

'And the next morning, you hit the little blue bottle that you know. You have a few good belches smelling of whiskey. A hot bath, then an icy shower, and the world is nice and clean again. You're happy as can be to find yourself back in your tidy house, the streets swept, the car riding quietly, the office air-conditioned. And life is beautiful, Julius!'

Maigret was looking at the two couples over in the corner, near the jukebox, who were looking back at them.

In short, it was so that life could be beautiful that Bessie was dead!

8. The Black Man Speaks Up

All five of them were there, in the blue prison uniforms, out in the second-storey colonnade. The much-laundered clothing had turned the same blue as sardine nets, the same blue as the morning sky you see each day as pure as ever.

In a shady recess there still lingered a little coolness from the night and the dawn, but crossing the line of light meant entering burning waves that seared the skin.

Soon, when the sun would be at its zenith in the sky, one of the five men might stand accused of manslaughter or murder.

Were they thinking about that? And were those of them who knew themselves to be innocent wondering who among them had killed? Or did they know and had they remained silent only through friendship or solidarity?

What was striking was their isolation.

They belonged to the same base, the same unit. They had gone out drinking, had fun together and called one another by their first names.

Yet at their first appearance before the coroner, invisible walls had divided them and made them strangers.

Most of the time, they avoided looking at one another, and when they happened to do so the look in their eyes was grave and heavy with bitterness or suspicion.

Sometimes they brushed up against one another, elbow to elbow, yet without making any real contact.

Among these men, however, there still existed bonds that Maigret had sensed from the first day and was now beginning to understand.

For example, they divided into two distinct groups, not only when out on leave, but back in the barracks as well.

Sergeant Ward and Dan Mullins formed one of these groups. They were the oldest – it was tempting to call them the grown-ups – and next to them the other three looked like rookies, in the junior class.

Like new pupils, those three had an aura of clumsiness, indecision, and they looked at their colleagues with envious admiration.

Yet the thickest and most impenetrable wall was between Ward and Mullins. Could Ward forget that Mullins had possessed Bessie almost before his eyes, in the musician's kitchen, and that this was doubtless the last embrace she had known?

To have her, it was he who had paid the price. He had promised to get a divorce, which meant he would be cut off from his children. He had wagered everything in the game, while his friend had simply gazed at her with his bedroom eyes.

Did Ward not have more serious suspicions about Mullins? Was it not believable that he had spoken in good faith about having secretly been drugged?

He had fallen abruptly asleep, and his pride as a drinking man kept him from admitting that the cause was alcohol. He did not know how long he had slept. Maigret had made an amusing observation on this point. Whenever the coroner or the attorney had asked the men to be more specific about the time, they had wound up saying, 'I didn't have a watch on.'

That had reminded Maigret of his military service, back when soldiers earned a pittance and when, after a few weeks, every watch in the regiment was in a pawnshop.

What proved to Ward that Mullins had remained sitting next to him in the car?

Maigret had put the matter to Cole, who knew about such things because of his job.

'Couldn't the musician have had marijuana cigarettes at his place?'

'First of all, I'm fairly certain he did not. Secondly, had he had some, they would not have plunged Ward into the deep sleep he described. On the contrary, he would have felt abnormally energized.'

And didn't Mullins, for his part, suspect Ward of having slipped off while he was asleep to go up to the railway tracks?

No look of hatred or reproach was ever observed between them, however. Each of them, frowning hard, seemed stubbornly to be trying to solve the problem on his own.

In the junior class, Van Fleet was the most nervous. That morning, he had the eyes of someone who has not slept all night or who has been crying for a long time.

His gaze was fixed and anxious. He seemed to sense an imminent misfortune, and his nails were bitten to the quick. He kept chewing on them at times without thinking, would stop abruptly when he realized it, then try to compose himself.

O'Neil, stubborn and sullen, still resembled a good student who has been unjustly punished, and he was the only one of the five awkwardly wearing a prison uniform too big for him.

As for Wo Lee, there was something pure in his attitude, his eyes, his delicate features, that made you want to treat him like a child.

'Last day!' a joyous voice exclaimed at Maigret's ear, making him jump.

It was a juror, the oldest one, who looked like an etching: his eyes, surrounded by a thousand fine, deep wrinkles, sparkled with both kindness and mischief. He had seen Maigret attend the inquest so faithfully and with such passionate interest that he must have thought him disappointed that it was ending already.

'The last day, yes.'

Did the old man, who seemed so carefree, already have his own opinion of the case? Van Fleet, who was the closest suspect and had overheard him, began to chew his nails again, while Sergeant Ward stared sombrely at the heavy man with the foreign accent who seemed to take an interest in him, God knows why.

They were all freshly shaven. Ward had even had his hair cut: it had been left shorter than usual around the nape and ears, so that the white skin there stood out against his suntan.

Something unusual was going on. It was twenty to ten, and Ezekiel had not yet summoned the jurors to the hearing.

He was not out in the arcade but downstairs, in the shade, near the lawn, smoking his pipe in front of a closed door.

No one had seen the coroner, or the attorney, or O'Rourke, who were usually bustling about in the corridors.

The regulars had taken their places in the courtroom as of nine thirty and then had drifted out one after the other, leaving a hat or some other object to save their seats. They gazed down on Ezekiel. Some of them went downstairs for a Coca-Cola. The black woman with the baby spoke to Maigret, but he did not understand what she said and simply smiled at her, then tickled the child's chin with one finger.

He went downstairs too, saw there was a meeting going on in the coroner's glassed-in office and recognized O'Rourke, who was on the phone.

He slipped a nickel into the slot of the red machine and drank his first Coca-Cola of the morning from the bottle. From below, he continued to watch the five men leaning on the balustrade upstairs.

That is when he took a piece of paper from his wallet and scribbled something on it. There was a vendor of newspapers and postcards in the arcade who also sold envelopes, so Maigret bought one, slipped his paper inside, closed it and wrote O'Rourke's name on the outside.

There was an increasing sense of impatience and a certain uneasiness. Everyone had finally noticed the door behind which the officials were closeted and from which emerged the occasional harried deputy, who would rush off to another office.

At last a light-coloured car stopped in front of the arcade, and a short, squat man crossed the patio, going towards the sheriff's office. They must have been watching for him, because O'Rourke ran to meet him and led him back to the office. The door closed behind them.

Finally, at five to ten, with a last puff on his pipe, Ezekiel called out his traditional: 'Members of the jury!'

Everyone sat down. The coroner tried different positions in his armchair and adjusted the microphone. Ezekiel fiddled for a moment with the air-conditioner buttons and went to shut the venetian blinds.

'Angelino Potzi!'

O'Rourke looked around for Maigret and winked at him. Harold Mitchell, sitting a little way off, noticed the gesture and glowered.

'Are you a food retailer and supplier for the Air Force base?'

'I provide food and drink for the officers' mess and the non-coms' mess.'

His background was Italian, and he still had an accent. He was overheated from his hurried arrival and mopped his brow constantly, looking around with curiosity.

'Do you know anything about the death of Bessie Mitchell? Have you heard anything about this inquest?'

'No, sir. I arrived one hour ago from Los Angeles, where I went with one of my trucks to pick up some produce. My wife told me that someone had telephoned several times during the night to ask if I'd got home. A little while ago, just when I'd showered and was about to go to bed, a man from the sheriff arrived.'

'What have you been doing since the morning of July 28?'

'When I left the base, where I had some orders to pick up—'

'Just a moment. Where did you spend the night of July 27 to July 28?'

'In Nogales, on the Mexican side. I had just bought two truckloads of cantaloupes and one truckload of vegetables. I spent part of the night with my suppliers, as we often do.'

'Did you have a lot to drink?'

'Not much. We played poker.'

'Did anything else happen?'

'We went up to have a drink in the red-light district, and while my vehicle was parked outside, a car must have run into it, because I found one fender damaged.'

'Describe your vehicle.'

'It's a beige Pontiac, which I bought used about a week ago.'

'Did you know that the tyres had been bought on credit?'

'I did not. I often buy and resell vehicles. Not so much for profit as to do someone a favour.'

'At what time did you begin driving back to Tucson?'

'It must have been about three a.m. when I drove through the border gate. I chatted for a moment with the immigration agent, who knows me well.'

He had kept the European habit of gesticulating while speaking and kept looking at all the people around him, as if he did not yet understand what was wanted of him.

'Were you alone in the car?'

'Yes, sir. As I approached Tucson Airport I saw someone signalling me to stop. I figured he was hitchhiking and was sorry he hadn't turned up earlier, because I would have had some company.'

'What time was that?'

'I wasn't driving fast. It must have been a little past four.'

'Was it daylight?'

'Not yet. But the sky wasn't black any more.'

'Turn around and tell us which of these men waved you down like that.'

Potzi did not hesitate.

'It was the Chinese man!'

'Was he alone by the highway?'

'Yes, sir.'

'How was he dressed?'

'I think he was wearing a purplish or violet shirt.'

'Did you see any vehicles on your way to Tucson?'

'Yes, I did, sir, about two miles farther on.'

'Headed towards Nogales?'

'Yes. A Chevrolet was parked by the side of the road, in front of a telegraph pole. Its lights weren't on, and for a moment I thought it was an accident, because the front bumper was almost touching the pole.'

'Did you notice anyone inside it?'

'It was too dark.'

'What did Corporal Wo Lee say when you stopped?'

'He asked me if I would wait a moment for his two friends, who would be arriving any second. He added that all three of them were from the base, and I replied that I was just on my way there. I thought the two others had gone off a moment to relieve themselves.'

'Did you wait a long time?'

'It seemed long to me, yes.'

'About how many minutes?'

'Maybe three or four. The corporal shouted some names, using his hands like a megaphone, turned towards the railway tracks.'

'Could you see the tracks?'

'No, but I often drive that route and I know where they pass.'

'Did Wo Lee walk towards the tracks?'

'No. I could tell he'd decided to leave without his friends if they didn't show up right away.'

'He was inside the vehicle?'

'He stayed outside, leaning on the front fender.'

'Was that the fender that had been damaged in Nogales?'

'Yes, sir.'

Maigret understood. The police must have found paint chips on the highway, which was why the three men had been asked if the car that brought them back to the base showed signs of an accident.

'What happened next?'

'Nothing. The other two arrived. We heard their footsteps first.'

'Coming from the direction of the tracks?'

'Yes.'

'What did they say?'

'Nothing. They got right in the car.'

'Did they sit in the back?'

'One of the two sat in back with the Chinese. The other sat next to me.'

He turned around and, without being asked, pointed at O'Neil.

'That's the one who was in front.'

'Did he chat with you?'

'No. He was very red and breathing heavily. I thought he was drunk and had maybe just vomited.'

'They didn't talk among themselves?'

'No. To tell you the truth, I began to talk on my own.'

'All the way to the base?'

'Yes. I left them in the first courtyard, just after the barbed wire. I think the Chinese fellow was the only one to say thank you.'

'Did you find anything in your car afterwards?'

'No, sir. I took care of my business at the base and drove home. I often stay up all night. The driver came to get me with one of the trucks, and we headed out towards Los Angeles. We left there yesterday at noon. I haven't read the papers, because I've been real busy.'

'Any questions, members of the jury?'

They shook their heads, and Potzi, collecting the straw hat he had placed on the floor, went towards the exit.

'One moment. Would you be good enough to hold yourself for a little while yet at the disposal of the court?'

As there were no empty seats, Potzi stood in the doorway and lit a cigarette, thus drawing upon himself the thundering of Ezekiel.

Just when O'Rourke was standing up at last, the elderly black juror raised his hand as if at school.

'I would like for each of the five men to be asked, under oath, when he saw Bessie Mitchell, alive or dead, for the last time.'

Maigret shivered and looked at the juror with mingled astonishment and admiration. As O'Rourke sat back down, he turned towards his colleague with a look that said, 'Not so stupid, that old guy!'

Only the coroner seemed annoyed.

'Sergeant Ward!' he called.

And when the sergeant was seated before the chrome-plated microphone:

'You have heard the juror's question. I remind you that you are still under oath. When did you last see Bessie, alive or dead?'

'On July 28, in the afternoon, when Mr O'Rourke took me to the morgue to identify her.'

'When did you see her before that for the last time?'

'When she left the car with Sergeant Mullins.'

'When the car was stopped for the first time, on the right side of the highway?'

'Yes, sir.'

'When you left the car later to go and look for her, you did not see her?'

'No, sir.'

The black juror indicated that he was satisfied.

'Sergeant Mullins! I ask you the same question and remind you of the same caution. When did you see Bessie for the last time?'

'When she got out of the car with Ward, and they went off into the darkness.'

'During the first stop?'

'No, sir. The second one.'

'Meaning, when the car was already turned towards Tucson?'

'Yes, sir. I did not see her again after that.'

'Corporal Van Fleet.'

He was clearly at the breaking point. His nerves, for whatever reason, were beginning to give way, and the slightest shock would be enough to make him crumble. His face was red with blotches, his fingers twitched, and he hardly knew where to look.

'Did you hear the question?'

O'Rourke had leaned over the attorney, who addressed the witness.

'I emphasize the fact that you are testifying under oath and I remind you that perjury is a federal crime punishable by up to ten years in prison.'

He was a painful sight to see, like an injured cat being tortured by frenzied boys. For the first time, the tragic drama was striking home. At that very moment the black woman's baby began to cry. The coroner scowled impatiently. The mother tried in vain to hush the child. Twice Van Fleet opened his mouth to speak, and both times the baby wailed even more loudly, so that in the end the woman regretfully decided to leave the courtroom.

Then Pinky opened his mouth once more, and it remained open without producing a single sound. The silence seemed as long as Potzi's three-minute wait beside the highway. Everyone felt a desire to help the corporal, to whisper an answer to him or ask the coroner not to intimidate him any more.

O'Rourke bent down yet again to the attorney, who then rose and walked straight over to the witness stand, shaking a pencil at Van Fleet like a schoolteacher.

'Did you hear Mr Potzi's deposition? When he pulled over at the side of the highway, your friend Wo Lee was there, alone. Where were you?'

'In the desert.'

'Over by the railway tracks?'

'Yes.'

'On the railbed?'

He shook his head vigorously.

'No, sir. I swear I did not set foot on the tracks.'

'But, from where you were, couldn't you see them?'

No reply. Van Fleet looked everywhere and nowhere. Maigret sensed that he must have been making a huge effort not to turn around towards O'Neil.

His forehead was beaded with sweat, and he was biting his nails again.

'What did you see on the tracks?'

He did not answer, rigid with panic.

'In that case, answer the first question: when did you see Bessie, alive or dead, for the last time?'

The Dutchman's anguish was so telling that everyone's nerves felt the strain, and some people must have felt like shouting, 'Enough!'

'I said alive or dead . . . Did you hear me? Answer!'

Then Van Fleet shot to his feet and burst into tears, shaking his head convulsively.

'It wasn't me! It wasn't me!' he yelled, panting. 'I swear it! It wasn't me! . . .'

He was shaking from head to toe, in hysterics, his teeth chattering, and he gazed around the courtroom with eyes so lost they could not have seen a thing.

O'Rourke moved quickly to him and grasped one arm firmly to keep the young man from flinging himself to the floor. He led him that way to the door and handed him over to Gerald Conley, the stout deputy with the carved-grip revolver.

He spoke to the deputy in a low voice, then went to confer with the coroner.

The atmosphere was one of hesitation, indecision. The attorney joined the discussion with the coroner, which continued for a few moments. Then the men seemed to look around for someone. Hans Schmider, the plaster-mould technician, was brought in from the corridor, carrying a package.

Addressing the black juror, the coroner murmured, 'If you'll allow us, we will listen to this witness before asking the last two men your question. Step up, Schmider. Tell us what you discovered last night.'

'I went to the base with two men, and we searched through the rubbish waiting to be burned. The rubbish is piled up on some waste ground a little way from the barracks. We had to use flashlights. And this is what we found.'

From a cardboard box he withdrew a pair of shoes, rather battered, and showed that they had rubber heels.

'I compared these with the footprints. They are definitely the shoes that left the second set of prints.'

'Explain.'

'I call set number one the footprints that go approximately from the car to the railway tracks, more or less following the path of Bessie Mitchell. Set number two designates the prints that begin farther along the highway towards Nogales, ending at the same place, on the railway bed, not far from where the body was found.'

'Were you able to determine to whom these shoes belong?'

'No, sir.'

'Did you question the people at the base?'

'No, sir. There are around four thousand men there.'

'Thank you.'

Before leaving, Schmider placed the shoes on the attorney's table.

'Corporal Wo Lee.'

He walked over to the witness stand, and, once more, the microphone had to be lowered.

'Do not forget that you are testifying under oath. I ask you the same question I put to your comrades. When did you see Bessie Mitchell for the last time?'

He did not hesitate. He did, however, wait a beat, the way he usually did, as if mentally translating the question into his own language.

'When she left the car the second time.'

'You did not see her after that?'

'No, sir.'

'Didn't you hear her?' the attorney asked quickly, after prompting from O'Rourke.

This time, Wo Lee thought longer, staring at the floor for a moment, opening his clear eyes wide, with their lashes as long as a girl's.

'I am not sure, sir.'

He immediately looked over at O'Neil, with an air of asking forgiveness.

'What do you mean, exactly?'

'I heard some noises, as if people were arguing and shaking bushes.'

'When was that?'

'Maybe ten minutes before the car drove up.'

'You're talking about Mr Potzi's car?'

'Yes, sir.'

'You were by the highway?'

'I never left it.'

'Had it been a long time since you'd sent away the taxi?'

'Maybe half an hour.'

'Where were your friends?'

'When we let go of the taxi, we walked all together at first towards Nogales, as I told you. I believe we had made a mistake about the place and had stopped too close to the airfield. After a while, we turned around and we split up. I continued to walk along the highway. I heard Van Fleet about twenty yards into the desert, and O'Neil was farther off.'

'Over by the railway tracks?'

'Just about. At one point, there was some noise.'

'Did you recognize a woman's voice?'

'I don't know.'

'Did the noise last a long time?'

'No, sir, it was very short.'

'Did you hear either Van Fleet's voice, or O'Neil's?'

'I think so.'

'Which one?'

'O'Neil's.'

'What was he saying?'

'It was hard to tell. I think he was calling Van Fleet.'

'He called out that name?'

'No, sir. He called him Pinky, the way he usually did. Someone started to run. I thought I heard quiet talking. That's when I noticed a car coming from Nogales and stepped out into the highway to signal to it.'

'You knew that your friends would rejoin you?'

'I thought that when they heard the car stop, they would come.'

'Any questions, counsellor?'

The attorney shook his head.

'Members of the jury?'

They said no as well.

'Recess!'

9. The Sergeant's Hip Flask

Maigret tried in vain to stop O'Rourke as he went by. Preoccupied, the chief deputy sheriff had gone quickly past and shut himself up in what must have been his office, on the ground floor. The window there was open because of the heat, and an endless stream of people could be seen filing through during the recess.

Pinky was there, sitting in a chair near some green filing cabinets. He had been given a drink to calm him down.

O'Rourke and one of his men were talking to him gently, in a friendly way, and the corporal managed to smile wanly a few times.

Escorted by her brothers and sisters, the black woman was still walking up and down the corridors, her baby in her arms, and when the jurors were summoned, she was the first spectator to return to her seat.

In the end, the business had been conducted more or less as in France, except that there, the interrogations would have taken place in one of the offices of the Police Judiciaire, behind closed doors, instead of in public.

The jurors seemed more solemn, as if they could feel the hour of their greatest responsibility drawing nigh.

If the black juror had not asked his question, would the inquest have taken the same turn? Would O'Rourke have taken charge of the proceedings?

'Corporal Van Fleet.'

Now he looked like a boxer who has taken a real beating in the earlier rounds and who advances towards his adversary for the knock-out punch, so people watched him with some compassion.

They knew that he knew, and everyone wanted to learn the truth at last. At the same time, they were a little ashamed about the state to which he had necessarily been reduced.

The coroner left the job of polishing him off to the attorney, who rose once more to approach the witness, his pencil in hand.

'About ten minutes before the car arrived that would take all three of you back to the base, something happened on the railway tracks, and some noise was heard by Wo Lee from the highway. Did you hear anything?'

'Yes, sir.'

'Did you see something?'

'Yes, sir.'

'Exactly what happened?'

He had clearly decided to tell all. He was trying to find the right words and almost seemed on the verge of asking for help.

'Ted had already been lying with Bessie for a while . . .'

It was strange to hear him, at that precise moment, call O'Neil by his first name.

'I suppose I must have made some noise without meaning to.'

'How far away were you from the couple?'

'Five or six yards.'

'O'Neil knew you were there?'

'Yes.'

'It had been arranged between you?'

'Yes.'

'Who bought the hip flask, and when?'

'It was a little before the Penguin Bar closed for the night.'

'Was it bought along with the other bottles?'

'No.'

'Whose idea was it?'

'Ours.'

'You mean you and O'Neil.'

'Yes, sir.'

'With what intention did you purchase a bottle that could be slipped into a pocket, when you had been drinking all evening and would keep on drinking at the musician's place?'

'We wanted to get Bessie drunk, and Sergeant Ward wasn't letting her drink as much as she wanted.'

'Did you have any specific intentions as of that moment?'

'Maybe not specific ones.'

'You knew someone would suggest finishing up the night in Nogales?'

'There or elsewhere, it always happens in the same way.'

'In short, before you left the Penguin, which means before one in the morning, you knew what you wanted?'

'We were saying that we might have an opportunity.'

'Was Bessie aware of this?'

'She knew that Ted had gone to the Penguin several times to meet her.'

'Had you let Wo Lee in on the secret?'

'No, sir.'

'Who had the flask in his pocket?'

'O'Neil.'

'Who paid for it?'

'Both of us. I gave him two one-dollar bills. He put in the rest.'

'There was already another bottle in the car.'

'We didn't know beforehand if it would be left there. And besides, it was too big a bottle to hide.'

'When you left for Nogales and O'Neil wound up in the back with Bessie, did he try to take advantage of that?'

'I suppose.'

'Did he give her anything to drink?'

'It's possible. I didn't ask him about it.'

'If I understand correctly, it had suited you both perfectly to abandon Bessie in the desert.'

'Yes, sir.'

'Did the two of you discuss it?'

'We didn't need to, we understood each other.'

'Did you decide at that time to get rid of Wo Lee?'

'Yes, sir.'

'You did not anticipate that Ward and Mullins would go back out into the desert?'

'No, sir.'

'Did you assume that Bessie would go along with this?'

'She'd already had a lot to drink.'

'And you planned to have her drink more?'

'Yes, sir.'

Having come this far, he would now answer even the most awkward and embarrassing questions.

'How come it took you about half an hour to find Bessie Mitchell?'

'We must have stopped the taxi too soon. We'd been drinking, too. It's hard at night to recognize a particular place along the highway.'

'Both of you tried again to send Wo Lee back. And when you all turned around, you two were both walking in the desert.'

'Yes, sir.'

'Were you together?'

'O'Neil was on my right, about twenty yards off. I could hear his footsteps. Now and then he'd whistle softly to let me know where he was.'

'Did he find Bessie on the railway tracks?'

'No, sir. Close by.'

'Was she sleeping?'

'I don't know. I guess so.'

'Exactly what happened then?'

'I heard him talking softly to her and I realized that he was lying on the ground with her. At first she thought it was Sergeant Ward. Then she burst out laughing.'

'Did he give her some alcohol?'

'He must have, because I heard the sound of the empty bottle falling on pebbles, probably on the railbed.'

'What were you doing meanwhile?'

'I was going closer as quietly as possible.'

'Did O'Neil know this?'

'Probably.'

'Was this the agreement you both had?'

'More or less.'

'And that's when something unexpected happened?'

'Yes, sir. I must have been caught by a thorn bush, and that made some noise. Then Bessie started fighting and got furious. She shouted that now she understood, that we were dirty scum, that we took her for a whore, but that we were wrong. O'Neil tried to make her be quiet, because he was afraid that Corporal Wo Lee might hear her.'

'Did you go any closer?'

'No, sir. I didn't move. But she could see my outline. She was cursing us, promising to tell Ward, who'd punch us right in the face.'

He spoke in a monotone, amid absolute silence.

'Was O'Neil holding her around the torso?'

'She ordered him to let go of her, she was struggling. She finally fought free and started to run.'

'On the railway tracks?'

'Yes, sir. O'Neil ran after her. She could hardly stay on her feet and was weaving around. She tripped a couple of times on the wooden ties. She fell down.'

'And?'

'O'Neil shouted, "Are you there, Pinky?"'

'I went towards him and heard him grousing, "That bitch!"'

'He asked me to go and see if she was hurt. I told him to go himself because I didn't have the courage. I felt sick. I heard a car coming along the highway. Wo Lee called to us.'

'No one went to see what state Bessie was in?'

'O'Neil finally went over. He merely bent down towards her. He put his hand out but didn't touch her.'

'What did he say when he came back?'

'He said, "That's a dirty trick she's playing on us. She isn't moving."'

'Did you conclude that she was dead?' *!?!*

'I don't know. I couldn't ask him any more questions. The car was waiting for us. We could see its headlights. We could hear the driver's voice.'

'You never thought about the train?' *Yipes!*

'No, sir.'

'O'Neil didn't bring that up?'

'We didn't talk at all.'

'And back at the base?'

'No. We went to bed without saying a thing.'

'Any questions, members of the jury?'

No one moved.

'Sergeant O'Neil.'

The two men crossed paths near the witness stand without looking at each other.

'When did you see Bessie Mitchell for the last time?'

'When she fell on the tracks.'

'Did you bend down over her?'

'Yes, sir.'

'Was she hurt?'

'I thought I saw blood on one temple.'

'Did you conclude from this that she was dead?'

'I don't know, sir.'

'It never occurred to you to move her somewhere else?'

'I didn't have time, sir. The car was waiting.'

'You never thought about the train?'

For a moment, he hesitated.

'Not exactly.'

'When you'd found her near the tracks, was she sleeping?'

'Yes, sir. She woke up almost immediately.'

'What did you do?'

'I gave her something to drink.'

'Did you have sex with her?'

'I started to, sir.'

'What interrupted you?'

'She heard a noise. When she saw the vague shape of Corporal Van Fleet, she figured things out and began struggling, yelling abuse at me. I was afraid Wo Lee might hear. I tried to make her be quiet.'

'Did you hit her?'

'I don't think so. She was drunk. She was clawing at me, I was trying to make her listen to reason.'

'Did you intend to kill her to make her be quiet?'

'No, sir. She got away from me and started to run.'

'You've seen these shoes: do they belong to you?'

'Yes, sir. The next day I thought someone might find footprints in the sand, so I threw them away.'

'Any more questions?'

After O'Neil had left the stand, the coroner called out: 'Mr O'Rourke.'

He simply stood up without leaving his spot.

'I have nothing to add,' he said. 'Unless anyone has questions to ask me.'

His expression was modest, almost astonished, as if he'd

had nothing to do with what had just happened, and Maigret muttered between his teeth.

'Well, you sly old faker!'

Then, like a man at the end of his tether, the coroner read a formula placing the jury in the care of Ezekiel, who swore to prevent the jury from communicating with anyone whomsoever during the term of their deliberations.

The coroner then explained a few things to the five men and one woman, whom everyone watched disappear into another room as the oaken door closed behind them.

Out in the arcade, there again were the white shirts, the cigars and cigarettes, the bottles of Coca-Cola.

'I think you have plenty of time to go and have lunch,' announced O'Rourke to Maigret. 'Unless I'm much mistaken, they'll be at it for an hour or two.'

'Did you get my note?'

'Forgive me, I'd clean forgotten it . . .'

He drew the envelope from his pocket, tore it open and read a single word: O'Neil.

For an instant, his usual gently mocking smile faded as he considered his colleague.

'Had you also understood that he had not done it on purpose?'

Instead of answering, Maigret asked him a question.

'What will happen to him?'

'I wonder whether he can be accused of rape, since in the beginning, at least, the girl was willing. He did not hit her at all. There still remains, in any case, the charge of perjury.'

'The penalty for which is something like ten years?'

'Right. They're kids, damn kids, aren't they?'

They were both probably thinking about Pinky and his breakdown. All five young men were not far away. Sergeant Ward and Mullins were sneaking glances at each other, as if each one was angry with himself for having suspected the other.

Were they going to make peace, become friends again as before? Would they draw a curtain over that business in the kitchen?

After hesitating a moment, Ward accepted the cigarette that Mullins offered him, but did not speak to him right away.

Wo Lee had done what he could to reply honestly to the questions without incriminating his comrades. He stood by himself, leaning against a column, drinking a Coca-Cola someone had fetched for him.

Van Fleet was speaking in a low voice with Deputy Conley, as if he still felt the need to explain himself, while O'Neil, all alone, his face closed up tight, stared savagely at the patio, where the sprinklers were refreshing the lawn.

'Damn kids!' O'Rourke had called them. The chief deputy sheriff was now eager to begin a new investigation.

As if he could not see any way out of it, he suggested to Maigret, 'Shall we have a quick one?'

What was preventing the two of them from re-establishing their cordiality and good humour of the previous evening? They went off to the corner bar, where they found several faithful spectators from the first two days of the inquest. No one was discussing the case. Each of them was drinking alone.

On the shelves behind the bar, sunlight played along the bottles of all colours. Someone had slipped a nickel into the jukebox. A ceiling fan rumbled above the bar; cars drove by outside, sleek and gleaming.

'Sometimes,' began Maigret in a hesitant voice, 'a person can feel constricted in ready-made clothes that are too tight in the armholes. Sometimes, even, that tightness becomes unbearable and the person wants to tear everything off.'

He emptied his glass in one go, ordered another one. He remembered what Harry Cole had confided to him, and thought of the thousands, the hundreds of thousands of men in the thousands of bars, who, all at the same time, were methodically drowning the same nostalgia, the same impossible need, and who the next morning, with the help of a shower and the stomach-settling blue bottle, would once again become decent men untrammelled by ghosts.

'Accidents are inevitable,' sighed O'Rourke, carefully cutting the tip of a cigar.

If Bessie hadn't heard any noise . . . If she hadn't raved drunkenly that they were treating her like a whore . . .

Five men and a woman – a few elderly folks, a black fellow, an Indian with a wooden leg – had come together under the watchful eye of Ezekiel and were trying, in the name of conscientious and organized society, to render a fair verdict.

'I've been looking for you for the past thirty minutes!' exclaimed Cole. 'How long would it take you, Julius, to pack your bags?'

'I don't know, why?'

'My colleague in Los Angeles is impatient to see you. One of the most famous gangsters in the West was shot down a few hours ago, just as he was leaving a Hollywood nightclub. My colleague is convinced that this will interest you. You have a direct flight in one hour.'

Maigret never saw Cole again, or O'Rourke, or the five Air Force men. He never learned the verdict. He did not even have time to buy the postcards with pictures of cacti flowering in the desert that he'd promised himself to send to his wife.

In the plane, he wrote to her on a pad of paper laid across his lap.

My dear Madame Maigret,

I'm having a wonderful trip, and my colleagues here are very kind to me. I think that Americans are nice to everyone. As for describing the country to you, it's rather difficult, but just imagine: for ten days now I have not worn a suit jacket, and I have a cowboy belt around my waist. Luckily, I did not let myself be pushed around, otherwise I'd be wearing boots and a broad-brimmed hat like the ones in Westerns.

By the way, I am in the Far West and at this moment am flying over mountains where you still see Indians with feathers on their heads.

What is beginning to seem unreal to me is our apartment on Boulevard Richard-Lenoir and the little corner café with the smell of calvados.

In two hours, I will be landing in the world of cinema stars and . . .

When he awoke, the pad had slipped from his knee; a stewardess, as pretty as a cover girl, was gently attaching his seat belt around his stomach.

'Los Angeles!' she announced.

He saw, at a slant – the plane was already banking – an immense expanse of white houses among green hills, at the edge of the ocean.

Whatever was he doing there?

Good Lord! After all the time he has been in the U.S., this is a really bizarre question to ask himself!

ASM III

7 April, 2017

INSPECTOR MAIGRET

OTHER TITLES IN THE SERIES

THE CELLARS OF THE MAJESTIC
GEORGES SIMENON

'Try to imagine a guest, a wealthy woman, staying at the Majestic with her husband, her son, a nurse and a governess… At six in the morning, she's strangled, not in her room, but in the basement locker room.'

Below stairs at a glamorous hotel on the Champs-Élysèes, the workers' lives are worlds away from the luxury enjoyed by the wealthy guests. When their worlds meet, Maigret discovers a tragic story of ambition, blackmail and unrequited love.

Translated by Howard Curtis

OTHER TITLES IN THE SERIES

THE JUDGE'S HOUSE
GEORGES SIMENON

'He went out, lit his pipe and walked slowly to the harbour. He could hear scurrying footsteps behind him. The sea was becoming swollen. The beams of the lighthouses joined in the sky. The moon had just risen and the judge's house emerged from the darkness, all white, a crude, livid, unreal white.'

Exiled from the Police Judiciare in Paris, Maigret bides his time in a remote coastal town in France. There, among the lighthouses, mussel farms and the eerie wail of foghorns, he discovers that a community's loyalties hide unpleasant truths.

Translated by Howard Curtis

OTHER TITLES IN THE SERIES

SIGNED, PICPUS
GEORGES SIMENON

'"It's a matter of life and death!" he said.

A small, thin man, rather dull to look at, neither young nor old, exuding the stale smell of a bachelor who does not look after himself. He pulls his fingers and cracks his knuckles while telling his tale, the way a schoolboy recites his lesson.'

A mysterious note predicting the murder of a fortune-teller; a confused old man locked in a Paris apartment; a financier who goes fishing; a South American heiress... Maigret must make his way through a frustrating maze of clues, suspects and motives to find out what connects them.

Translated by David Coward

INSPECTOR MAIGRET

OTHER TITLES IN THE SERIES

INSPECTOR CADAVER
GEORGES SIMENON

'To everyone, even the old ladies hiding behind their quivering curtains, even the kids just now who had turned to stare after they had passed him, he was the intruder, the undesirable.'

Asked to help a friend in trouble, Maigret arrives in a small provincial town where curtains twitch and gossip is rife. He also finds himself facing an unexpected adversary: the pale, shifty ex-policeman they call 'Inspector Cadaver'.

Translated by William Hobson

OTHER TITLES IN THE SERIES

FÉLICIE
GEORGES SIMENON

'In his mind's eye he would see that slim figure in the striking clothes, those wide eyes the colour of forget-me-not, the pert nose and especially the hat, that giddy, crimson bonnet perched on the top of her head with a bronze-green feather shaped like a blade stuck in it.'

Investigating the death of a retired sailor on the outskirts of Paris, Maigret meets his match in the form of the old man's housekeeper: the sharp-witted, enigmatic and elusive Félicie.

Translated by David Coward

OTHER TITLES IN THE SERIES

Pietr the Latvian

The Late Monsieur Gallet

The Hanged Man of Saint-Pholien

The Carter of *La Providence*

The Yellow Dog

Night at the Crossroads

A Crime in Holland

The Grand Banks Café

A Man's Head

The Dancer at the Gai-Moulin

The Two-Penny Bar

The Shadow Puppet

The Saint-Fiacre Affair

Mr Hire's Engagement

The Flemish House

The Madman of Bergerac

The Misty Harbour

Liberty Bar

Lock No. 1

Maigret

Cécile is Dead

The Cellars of the Majestic

The Judge's House

Signed, Picpus

Inspector Cadaver

Félicie

Maigret Gets Angry

Maigret in New York

Maigret's Holiday

Maigret's Dead Man

Maigret's First Case

My Friend Maigret

Maigret at the Coroner's

Maigret and the Old Lady

Madame Maigret's Friend

Maigret's Memoirs

Maigret at Picratt's

And more to follow

www.penguin.com